THE LAST AMERICAN MARTYR

by

Tom Winton

ISBN   1466254416

EAN   978-1466254411

To my wife, Blanche, for all her sacrifices and undying optimism.

Special thanks to Carole Yates Williams and Diane Nelson for all their help.

Chapter 1

Most folks in White Pine thought the man they knew as Darius McClure was quite eccentric, at the very least a borderline hermit. That in itself was quite odd since most residents of this rural northern Maine town put such a high premium on their own sense of seclusion. After all, more than a few locals had been known to wag or aim a twelve-gauge in order to preserve their own privacy. Occasionally, they pulled the trigger.

Everybody in White Pine knew that Clyde Therault, the town's most industrious burglar, and Norm Flagg, a fifth generation townie with a penchant for peeking in windows, both mysteriously vanished within a period of two years. Both men, who lived alone, were out of the picture for weeks before the regulars at Edna's Country Café realized they were missing. Since none of the townsfolk had any great love for either of the culprits, the revelation of their sudden departure was quickly forgotten, or simply no longer mentioned.

Curtis Bass, the town's part-time constable, quickly wrote off Therault and Flagg's disappearances as just that, disappearances. The gladly accepted consensus, though nobody actually believed it, was that the two were probably killed in hunting or snowmobile accidents somewhere deep in these North Woods.

But it was different with Darius McClure. Nobody really disliked him. How could they? Nobody really knew him. The only time anyone ever saw him was when he drove his maroon Subaru through the village, usually heading to or from the dirt logging roads that run deep into the endless pine forests up here. Most folks assumed he went there to hunt, maybe poach a deer or a moose, although nobody ever saw him come back with either.

But I know better. I was his mailman. And after a while, I'm proud to say, I had the good fortune of becoming his friend. I was the only one in these parts who ever got to know Darius. I knew well and good he didn't go out on those logging roads to poach. He only went there to jog. Sixty years old and he still did three miles a day, five times a week.

Despite his exercise regimen, he did like to swizzle a few beers every afternoon. He used to tell me, "Jake, I've always been a morning creature. When first light shows and the wildlife are most active, that's the only time of day I have even a semblance of hope for this damaged planet. By mid-afternoon, whatever inkling of optimism I may have had always fades. The earth seems to slow on its axis, and it's time for me to self-sedate."

Along with his beer, Darius liked his cigarettes too. Claiming to be "a judicious smoker," he usually stayed within his quota of ten per day. But the real kicker was, despite his vices, he was a self-proclaimed "pisca/vegetarian." That's what he called himself because, for the most part, he ate only fish and vegetables. Nobody else knew that either. If they had, hunting would have been ruled out and people *really* would have wondered what he was up to on those logging roads.

I must admit, when he first showed up, I was as curious about Darius as everyone else, probably more so since I went by his isolated trailer five times a week. Why would anyone from "away," especially a man getting on in his years, come to a place like White Pine? It's so remote up here that most every township within fifty miles is identified by a number instead of a name. Virtually no one lives in places like T13 R10 WELS, T13 R11 WELS, and so on, and so on. Why would Darius come up here, buy Norm Flagg's abandoned trailer for past due taxes, and hunker down all alone?

The first year I delivered his mail out on Split Branch Road, Darius and I rarely exchanged a word. Oh sure, if he was outside blowing snow, cutting grass, or washing his Subaru, we'd give each other a quick nod or wave. A few times, when I couldn't fit into his mailbox an unusually large batch of those books he was always getting, we exchanged polite hellos at his door. But that was it. Even if he wanted to talk, his yappy little terrier, "Solace," made it nearly impossible.

At first I couldn't fathom why anybody would call such a hyped-up Jack Russell "Solace." A short time later, I would fully understand. As time went on, I learned many more things from Darius McClure. Things that never entered my mind before I met him and never would had I not. Things like why an aging man who'd once been so gregarious and full of life would divorce himself from all of society.

Darius' place was the last stop on my route, way at the end of Split Branch, atop a small hill. The last half of that godforsaken dirt road is so full of ruts and holes, the fillings in your teeth chatter loose if you dare drive too fast. Steering along that thing is a full-body workout--you're constantly zigging and zagging, tapping the accelerator, and stomping the brake. When there was a heavy snow, or in the spring during mud season, after two feet of frozen earth thawed, there were days I couldn't even attempt to deliver Darius' mail. That road is nothing more than a two-mile, bone-shaking swath; meandering through trees so dark, dense, and imposing, you sometimes feel imprisoned.

The first time I ever shared anything more than a hint of recognition with Darius back there, was in May of 2010. Lucky for him it was one of those days when his books wouldn't fit in the mailbox.

I pulled into his unpaved driveway, parked behind his Outback, and killed the engine. As I reached for his Publisher's Weekly and the books, I heard the loud, grating buzz of a chainsaw coming from the tree line behind the trailer. Darius was obviously doing some work there. Being a fine, crisp spring day, and since the front door was wide open behind the screen door, I figured I'd just leave everything right there.

After plunking the books on the wooden entry deck, I started back down the steps. Again I heard the rising whine a chainsaw makes after severing a thick branch. That in itself was no big deal. But then the machine shut off abruptly, and that was odd. Next came the telltale cracking of smaller limbs, as a far heftier one made its way to the forest floor. There was a thud. Then there was a holler.

Echoing through the woods in all directions, Darius yelled, "Ohhhh Shhhhhit! At the same time, as if on command, Solace started raising all sorts of holy-hell back there. This wasn't the usual incessant barking and yapping she'd do whenever I pulled up to the mailbox or came to the door. This sounded like an entire pack of crazed terriers had just treed an animal but with three times the urgency and squealing.

Beating heels around the trailer, I saw Darius back in the trees, hanging from a thick pine limb about thirty feet up. With his back to me, legs flailing wildly, he yelled at Solace to "GET THE HELL OUT OF THE WAY." It was obvious his arms were about to give out.

"HOLD ON, MISTER McCLURE!" I shouted, tromping through a shady maze of thick tree trunks, trying not to trip on the undergrowth and bed of winter-fallen branches, "I'LL HELP YOU!"

"The ladder," he croaked now, his voice quickly losing strength, "it's lying in front of me."

His defeated tone told me he couldn't hold on much longer. This was one thick limb he was clutching. Unlike hanging from a bar, he couldn't wrap his fingers around it for a better grip. This was all palms and wrists.

In a voice just short of a shout, yet calm as I could be in such a circumstance, I said, "Don't you worry! Just hang on there!" Then, bending down to pick up the fully-extended aluminum ladder, "I'll have this back up in three seconds."

A couple of rungs at the far end were tangled in a small evergreen, but I wasn't about to tell Darius that. There wasn't enough time to run to the end of the ladder, undo the thing, then come back and raise it. I had no choice. It was like lifting an impossibly long lever with a boulder on the far end.

Here I was, straining to dislodge the cumbersome monstrosity, and Solace was only adding to the chaos with all her yelping, howling, and jumping around. Hot adrenaline coursed the veins in both my arms as if I'd main-lined it. My hands trembled uncontrollably and my biceps strained, but somehow I managed to free the thing. Under less urgent conditions, I could never have done it.

In a voice so low, exhausted, and meshed with defeat, I barely heard Darius up there saying, "I can't hold on any longer. Get out of the way, now! I'm going to drop."

"Nope! Here it is!" I said, guiding the ladder up to the limb, alongside his right hand. "Put your right foot on the nearest rung. Ahhh yup, that's it. Now pull your body weight onto it and grab the ladder. I'm holding onto it. Don't worry, it isn't going anywhere. That's it...you've got it."

Ever so slowly, Darius lowered himself. The thirty-foot ladder bowed and danced dangerously under his weight. My hands began to cramp, but I held on with all I had left. Solace's frantic, desperate barks kept echoing through the woods.

With each rung Darius descended, the whole thing wobbled, imperiling his life. After each uncertain step he hugged the rails like a long-lost lover until it stopped moving. The two inches of contact the end of the ladder made with the limb shortened with his every step. If it had gotten to the point where it tottered just a wee bit more, or it slid a few inches along the slick pine limb, it would have been all over. Three men couldn't have stopped it from coming down.

Darius was one exhausted man when he stepped on the ground.

"Terra firma," he said, dropping his head, still leaning on the ladder, his lungs working as if he'd been dunked underwater far too long, "Thought I'd never stand on solid ground again. Thought for sure it was time for the old dirt nap."

He then looked down at Solace, jumping and clawing at his thighs. "OK, OK, girl, come on up." Extending his scratched red palms up and out, the terrier elevated to them as if on springs. "Alright, alright," he said as the relieved dog slobbered his face.

"Thanks for helping me out," he said, extending his right hand to me, hanging on to the wriggling dog with the other. "I'm sorry, you've been delivering my mail for months now, and I still don't know your name."

"Jake...Jake Snow," I said, and as we shook hands, I did a quick study of his face.

Every time I'd gotten a quick glimpse of him in the past, when I'd handed him his books and mail through a partially opened doorway, I'd always thought he looked familiar for some reason. But I couldn't, for the life of me, figure out why. Eventually, I just assumed that someone I knew, or had known, must have had similar features. But his face was not all that ordinary. Despite his age, you'd still have to consider him somewhat handsome. And though his eyes seemed a bit tired after what he'd just been through, they jumped right out at you. He had eyes that nobody would forget. They were pale blue like the shallows of a tropical ocean, and they belied his age as much as his lean, taut body did.

As I let go of his hand I said, "Hey, you don't have to thank me. I'm just glad as hell I happened along at the right time."

"Me too...*I suppose*. No...don't take that literally, I'm just kidding. Thank you *very* much."

Now that he was catching his breath, he studied *me* a bit more closely. As he assessed my face, he asked, "Have you got time for a beer, Jake Snow?"

Before the three of us filed into his trailer, I picked up Darius' books and magazine from the deck. Once we were inside he asked me to have a seat, then went into the adjoining kitchen to pour Solace some fresh water and to fetch us two cold brews.

I'd been inside his trailer a few times before, when Norm Flagg was living in it. When Flagg was there the place was filthy and a shambles. Food-encrusted dishes were strewn everywhere like a scattered collection of drab, round frescoes. Soiled clothes were all over the thin carpet, dropped where they had been shed. Two pillows, gray with grime, laid to rest atop a worn and filthy sofa. The only things Flagg had on the paneled walls were a few naked center-folds from cheap girlie magazines and a one-eyed deer head that looked like it had been through one too many garage sales.

But now the place was much different. The furnishings were again sparse and inexpensive, but everything was immaculate. The second thing to hit me when I walked in this time was Darius' books. Three of the living room walls were lined with hip-high, shelves full of them. On the back wall, beneath a window looking into the forest where Darius had almost bought it minutes earlier, were two blue recliners. A table and lamp sat between them. On the table were an empty ashtray and a well-worn, hardcover copy of "A People's History of the United States." Though I'd never heard of the book before, I had delivered to the White Pine Library copies of Publisher's Weekly, like the ones neatly stacked beneath the table.

As I peered around the room some more, I noticed something else. Hanging just to the right of the front window was a thin-framed photograph of a very attractive young lady. Dressed like they did back in the 1960's, she had long, sleek, black hair, parted in the middle. Her face was one to die for. Next to that photograph, in a much larger frame, was the front page of a newspaper. There was a picture on that too, a large one. From where I sat, across the narrow room, it looked like Darius, shaking hands with another man.

I got up out of the chair, went over to it, and took a closer look. It was Darius alright, on the front page of the New York Times. Dressed in a suit and tie, he was receiving an award.

Hearing the first beer can pop and fizz in the kitchen by now, feeling like a snoop, I quickly read the headline. It said, "Nobel Prize Goes to Controversial Author Thomas Soles."

I'll be a son of a gun! I thought. I knew he looked familiar!

Then I scurried back across the room and fell back into the recliner just as Darius McClure/Thomas Soles returned with two beers.

Chapter 2

"I hope Busch Light works for you." he said, handing me an ice cold one.

"Sure...sure, that's great," I said, struggling to sound nonchalant. But that name, "Thomas Soles," kept echoing inside my head along with a stream of questions. *What the hell is this all about? What's he doing here, in a tiny, isolated town like White Pine? Why's he using an alias? What...*

McClure/Soles sat down and lit a cigarette. Then he got right up again, turned on the ceiling fan just above us, and sat back down. He looked across the table between us and said, "Thanks again for saving my life, Jake. Another minute...it would have been all over."

I detected in his words a slight, time-worn, New York accent. Many years and miles had probably passed since its inception, but it was a dialect, and it would fit somebody named Thomas Soles far better than it would a Darius McClure.

"You're more than welcome, Mister McClure." I said, feeling a little ridiculous calling him that now. "Anybody else would have done the same thing."

"Yes...maybe," he said. Then he paused as if he was trying and failing to think of one person he knew who would have helped him.

"I don't believe in fate, destiny, or any of that bunk," he went on, "but you happened along at the precise moment I was hanging on for my life. Heh, heh...no pun intended."

Only slightly creased at the corners, those blue eyes then lit up like a teenager's on prom night. Beneath the longish silver hair that obscured part of his forehead, I swear, those eyes talked. Looking back, knowing him as well as I do now, I realize they were saying, "I've seen most of what this world has to offer, Jake. There isn't much that has gotten by me. I've been alone for a long time now, and I'm eager to share what I've learned with someone like you. But for now, for this moment, I'm just damned glad you're here. I think you and I just might

8

become friends, but I have to be careful...very careful. I'm sorry."

"Mister McClure," I said, "I don't want to cross any boundaries here, you know, sound disrespectful or anything, but you've got to be more careful next time. You're never supposed to fully extend a ladder, barely secure it thirty feet up then climb to the top."

"I appreciate your concern," he said, "and you're a hundred percent right. I don't have a whole hell of a lot of experience with such things." He tapped his cigarette in the ashtray twice then went on. "You know...most people, particularly folks my age, don't like to admit when they're wrong. Politics, religion, socio-economic views, it doesn't matter. Nobody wants to fess up to being wrong about anything anymore. Despite all my typical human shortcomings, I like to think I'm smarter than that. I sure *hope* I'm intelligent enough to know when I'm wrong and humble enough to admit it. Hell, the older *I* get, the more I realize how little I actually do know. There's an awful lot of gray area in this business we call *life*. It's very unfortunate, Jake, but most people can't see beyond the black or the white. They just can't seem to get past the perceptions they've cemented in their minds."

At this point I began to wonder why this mysterious man was getting into such a heavy spiel. Yet at the same time, I welcomed his wise words. He didn't know me from Adam but, as he opened up to me, it somehow felt very natural. It seemed as if I had known him far longer than I actually had.

"I'm sorry for ranting," he said, punching out his smoke. "I've been alone here for quite some time now."

"You know, Mister McClure, it's really weird..."

"Please," he interrupted, shaking his head and waving one hand as if he were dusting the air, "please, call me Darius."

"OK...Darius, sure. Like I was saying, it's really weird. Most of the folks here in White Pine, I've known all my life. Good people, for the most part. But I've known you, what, fifteen minutes, and here I am feeling as if I know you better than any of them. Is that crazy or what?"

He looked through the window straight in front of us, surveying the deep green pines and blue sky above. A small smile, a nostalgic smile, found its way to his mouth. Then he peered into his near empty beer can as if he were searching for the perfect response in there. After swishing the contents around once or twice he looked back at me.

"Funny you say that, Jake," he said, still wearing that subtle smile, "because when I was a young man, back in New York during the late sixties and early seventies, my friends and I made a full-time job out of chasing the ladies. Whew! What a time that was to be young--the best. Anyway, in the course of seven, maybe eight years, we must have hit every club and disco from Manhattan to the Hamptons. OK, that's a stretch, but you get my drift. What I'm trying to say is I met an awful lot of girls in those places. And I can't *count* the times when, after talking to them for just ten minutes or so, they said almost the exact same thing you just did. You know, something like, this is weird, but I just met you and I feel like I've know you for a long time. Every time I heard that, it was music to my ears. I was a very fortunate young man to be able to communicate the way I did."

With that his eyes fell again to the now empty can, and he said, "How about another, Jake?"

I checked my watch: three-thirty. Kyle, the postmaster and only other employee at our tiny White Pine Post Office, would be closing up in half an hour. But I didn't want to leave quite yet. I had a key to the PO, and numerous times before I had let myself in and locked up when I left.

"Sure, I'll have another. That would be great." Then I pulled out my cell and said, "Just let me call the office, tell the head-honcho I'm going to be a bit late."

"Go right ahead. I want to get Solace here a slice of raw carrot too. She loves them. Be right back."

Just as I finished the call, Darius came back into the paneled room. He saw me looking in the direction of that framed newspaper. After glancing at the article himself, he hesitated for a split-second. Then he handed me one of the cold beers and sat back down. He lit another Carlton, took a swig of the beer, and said, "Well...I guess the proverbial cat is out of the bag now."

10

Talk about getting caught with your mitts in the old cookie jar! I hadn't the foggiest where this was going from here. I'd never felt so uncomfortable in my life. Maybe, I thought, just maybe, I should get out of this chair, make up some bullshit excuse, tell him, Oh, I just remembered I have to blah, blah, blah, and then hit the bricks. I squirmed a few times, cleared my throat, and tried to hold onto one of the few ridiculous options racing through my mind. I don't smoke, but I came damn close to asking him for a cigarette. I'd have done anything to fill those long, silent seconds.

But finally Thomas Soles, Nobel Prize laureate, broke the silence. With Solace the terrier now on his lap licking the bottom of his moist can, he turned to me and said, "Jake, from here on out, why don't you just call me Tom?"

Chapter 3

"Sure...I can call you Tom."

You have no idea how badly I wanted out of that trailer. I wished I was in my jeep, cannon-balling down Split Branch Road, bouncing off the inside roof. But what could I do? And in all honesty, how could I not be curious. It's not every day you get the opportunity to sit down with a Nobel laureate, particularly such an enigmatic one.

What Tom Soles said next, he said very slowly. I could tell he was weighing every word, trying them out inside his head before choosing just the right ones. Gently smoothing the tawny fur on Solace's back, he said, "Jake, it's been a long time since I've been able to confide in anybody other than my publisher, and as rarely as I speak to her, it's always on the telephone. I'm sixty-one years old now, and I don't know how much time I have left. I've been on the run for a year and a half now--on the lam, if you will. I've had very few meaningful, face-to-face conversations in all that time.

He paused for a sip, and probably to get his next words right. I wasn't sure I wanted to hear what he was preparing to tell me. I had a wife and two sons. I didn't want to get involved in anything I shouldn't. He'd been on the run for a year and a half! From what? What could this possibly be leading to? I had no answers, yet something kept me from bowing out of the conversation. And it continued.

"After all my years on this planet, I've become a pretty fair judge of character, Jake. And my instincts tell me you're a trustworthy person. That's a rare attribute, nowadays. Plus, you just saved my life. That alone is a damn good reason for feeling a certain affinity towards someone. Anyway...believe me; I never dreamed I'd open up to someone I've only known for such a short time. As I said, I'm getting closer to the dirt. It's very possible that I have far less time left than you might think. I desperately *need* to share my experiences and my fears, so here goes."

Tom then turned and nodded at the Times' article, "You know about the Nobel Prize, am I correct?"

"Well, yes, I saw the picture there and I was inquisitive. Ever since I started delivering your mail, I *thought* you looked familiar, but I couldn't quite place you. Of course, I've heard about you on the news and all."

"Are you interested in knowing more?"

"Are you in some kind of trouble with the law?"

"No, no," he said with a slow shake of the head and a melancholic smile, "my problems have nothing to do with breaking laws, only with speaking the truth."

"That's fine then, I suppose." I said, really knowing deep down it might not be, still feeling trouble could be attached to what he might tell me. "But why...what do you mean you've been on the lam?"

He turned away from me and again looked out the window alongside the article and the picture. As if searching for the answer to my question in those towering green pines or the endless blue space above them, he drew on his cigarette. After exhaling at the whirling fan above, he turned back to me and said, "This is going to sound kind of absurd, Jake, but when I say I've been on the lam, the run, whatever, I'm not even sure who, if anybody, is after me."

I must have looked at him as if he had four arms because a knowing look rose on his face and he chuckled before continuing.

"Do you like to read, Jake?"

"Sure, but mostly on my lunch breaks. Not much at home. I've got a wife with an endless honey-do list, two kids with more energy than the electric company, and six acres that also need constant attention. I'm always busy. But I do like reading...guys like Conroy and Jim Harrison, you know, fairly dramatic stuff."

"Well that's terrific. I'm glad you read because I have an idea. You see, telling you my entire story would take days, sitting here like this, and now we both know you don't have that kind of spare time. Don't get me wrong, I sure hope you continue stopping over here. I really enjoy talking with you.

Any time my car's out front you're more than welcome to come to the door. Anyway, back to my idea. How would you like to read a manuscript of mine? It's a memoir. Not a life story but it details what has happened to me since I won the prize. It explains everything you might want to know about this loony old man and why he's holing up in a thirty-five-year-old trailer in the North Maine Woods. Also, if you read it, you'll fully understand why I'm so desperate to share what I've been through."

"Yeah...Tom, I'd like that," I said, and I truly meant it.

He then put his palm up, spread his fingers, and punctuated some of his words as he spoke.

"Fine, then. I'll only give you one chapter at a time. I'd like to do it that way for two reasons, number one, you'll *have to* stop over and visit me from time to time—to return them and pick up more. The second reason is I'm in no way finished yet. I've still got, probably, a few months worth of work ahead of me. What do you say? Does that sound OK?"

By now my curiosity had gotten the best of me. I couldn't wait to get my hands on the manuscript. But I had to be honest. "Sure," I said, "I'd like that, very much. But like you said, if I feel like I'm going places I don't belong, I'll have to stop."

"Fair enough. That's fandamtastic, Jake! Hell, you might even find a few of the punctuation errors my editor is always chiding me about. If you do, I'd appreciate you circling them for me. You just might save me some of her good-natured heat."

Nodding my head in agreement, trying to appear capable, I didn't say anything.

"Yep, I know what you're thinking, Jake. People do think that anyone who's won the award is some sort of demigod. I don't know about all the rest of them, but I put my socks on each morning the same way everybody else does. Hell, I barely got through high school English, that's why my punctuation is only so-so. Of course, in all fairness to myself, I never was in that English class all that often."

Tom then jerked his thumb toward the narrow hallway and said, "Just like everyone else, I also straddle the toilet most mornings. Being so regular may be an achievement for somebody my age," he said, chuckling again, "but besides that, all I am is a simple man who's made some relevant observations and shed light on them in a simple book. That's it! I'm nothing more."

"Well," I said, "I've got a feeling there's a bit more to you than that."

"I don't know, maybe a bit more. Maybe the one small gift I was born with is an elevated degree of insightfulness. Someone, whose name now slips me, once did say, 'There's very little difference in the way most men think but that small difference can be huge.' Maybe he was on to something."

Tom drained the last of his beer, gently lowered Solace to the carpet, and said, "Wait here just a minute. I'll get the first chapter."

A few minutes later, as he walked me to my jeep, Tom Soles said, "Remember, if you begin to read anything that makes you feel uncomfortable, anything at all, just stop there and return the manuscript. I'll understand. And do me one more favor, if you would. Please don't tell anybody, not a soul, that my name is Thomas Soles."

I assured him I wouldn't and cranked up the engine. Then, as I went to put her in reverse, he leaned into the open window and said in a weary, yet relieved tone, "Thank you so much for doing this, Jake. You don't know how badly I wanted somebody to read this in case...in case something unforeseen happens to me."

Chapter 4

While negotiating the ruts and bumps on Split Branch Road, I kept stealing glances at the paper-clipped pages lying on the mail shelf beside me. It was a Saturday, and I knew darned well I'd never be able to wait till lunchtime Monday to dig into them.

So that night, after my wife, Sigrid, and the boys fell asleep, I grabbed my robe and tip-toed downstairs to the workshop. I threw a single log in the stove and settled into one of the two old upholstered chairs I keep down there for when my pals come over. Of course, I read every page of chapter one. From then on, for the next five months, I couldn't wait for Saturdays to roll around. Tom had said, at the very outset, he only wanted me to read one chapter a week. I wasn't going to push it. Maybe that in itself was an intended lesson for me. Maybe my new friend was teaching me the meaning of patience. I don't know, but I do know I learned an awful lot from his writings. The deeper I got into this manuscript the more I wanted to read on. Each paragraph *demanded* that I go onto the next. What follows here is verbatim what I read. You'll notice it had no title—Thomas Soles hadn't yet come up with one.

Had I, an unemployed doorman, never written that book, my life wouldn't have taken such a harrowing turn. Had it not sold so well, I wouldn't have needed to be on the lam like I have for so many months now. But I did write my book, and I'll pay for that until the last shovel of cold dirt is dumped over my grave. What's done is done. I can't undo a thing, even if I wanted to. On the other side of the coin, the words I strung together did have at least one positive effect. They seem to have broadened the entire world's perception of selfishness and greed. Many called my plainly-written book, a "revelator." Others were livid over the messages in its pages.

My thoughts about the unfair distribution of wealth in societies everywhere created a fiery uproar from pole to pole. There were massive marches and demonstrations in 17 different countries. From America to Zimbabwe, folks young and old turned out in astounding numbers. Their marching footsteps caused the entire planet to tremor. Class systems everywhere were suddenly being questioned, and in many places challenged. All this because of the thoughts I, a previously unpublished author, scrawled into Spiral notebooks at a Formica table in my Queens, New York tenement.

For two long years, I sat in that kitchen, staring out the window, searching for inspiration beyond the fire escape and all the sad brown buildings. Somehow, uncertain as I was, I did finish the book, and it was published. A year after that everything changed. It doesn't happen often, the odds are miniscule, but every once in a while a small person rises from the depths of obscurity and manages to shake the entire world. It happened in 2008 when I, dressed in a secondhand Goodwill suit, stepped onto the worldwide stage in Stockholm, Sweden and accepted the Nobel Prize for Literature. People everywhere were astounded that a first time author could be awarded such an honor, but the Nobel Committee felt that the book's world-wide impact was undeniable and unprecedented.

Alfred Bernhard Nobel, the inventor of dynamite who founded the prize, might have exploded in his casket that day had he known who the prize went to. The gold medal with his face on it, the diploma bearing a citation, and a million dollars went to me, Thomas Soles, a plain-speaking man who had railed against the very same system that made Nobel a very wealthy man.

Just like Alfred Nobel, I didn't have any secondary education. Well, actually, I did manage to complete two night courses at Queens College. After that, the Draft Board changed my plans. I wanted to go nights for one more term. At that point I'd have had enough credits to attend the city-funded New York college fulltime, tuition free. All I would have had to come up with was the cost of books. But, as it had been all my young life, the answer was a resounding NO. I spent the next 23 months in the U.S. Army, half that time in Viet Nam. I was in the infantry but have no desire to talk about that. As a matter of fact, I *need* not to talk about it.

After being discharged from the military in 1971, my money problems didn't get a whole lot better until thirty-six years later when my revolutionary book was picked up by a major publisher. Then things really changed. Money started coming at me from all directions.

A year later, to the blare of trumpets and the flash of cameras, I received a standing ovation at the Swedish Academy along with a check for a million dollars. One would have thought I'd be on easy street after that, but not me. Just as I'd done the previous year with my burgeoning book royalties, I planned to keep very little of the award money. Almost all of it would go to needy charities, again. All I wanted was *enough*. As a matter of fact, the title of the book that won me the Nobel Prize was *Enough is Enough*. Unfortunately, not everybody who read it agreed with the title or anything on its pages. At the very top of the system I had criticized, there were some extremely powerful people, concerned people, who were very, very upset.

Thirty-one thousand feet over the Atlantic Ocean, American Airlines flight 1402 was less than an hour from landing at Kennedy Airport. Pulling my uncertain eyes from the quivering wing outside the three-layered acrylic window, I said to my wife, Elaina, "Those drinks we had in London are helping, but I still don't like it."

"I must have told you fifty times, it's no big thing. You were so upset...for nothing."

"Just the same, if it was for anything less than the award, I wouldn't be up here."

"All right, Tom, we're almost home," Elaina said, closing her Newsweek, returning it to the pouch on the seat in front of her. After brushing one of her long black hairs from her jeans, she straightened up in her seat, looked past me at the clear blue October sky outside the window and said, "We need to talk about the money, you know."

"Aw come on, Elaina, not that. You know how I feel about that. I don't want to talk about it now, not here on a plane full of strangers."

"This isn't going away, Tom. Not this time. We've got to talk. I promised I wouldn't say another word about it until we left Stockholm, and I didn't. I didn't want to ruin everything."

Then she paused for a moment. Her perturbed look lost its edge and she failed to fight back a small smile. "Look Tom...OK...you know I'm still pinching myself. I can't believe you've actually won The Nobel Prize. Every time I think about it, I get goose bumps. Things like that just don't happen to people like us. All those uncertain hours, days, and months you spent in the kitchen writing your book...you didn't even think it would get published."

With that Elaina's eyes glazed over. She glanced at her neatly polished fingernails and sniffled. Then she turned back to me, cleared her throat, and changed the tone of her whisper again.

"Look, you've already given more than a million dollars in royalties to Greenpeace, Amnesty International, the ACLU, and all the rest. What about us? We're still in the same run-down apartment you grew up in. I'm still nursing forty-five hours a week at Queens General. We don't even have ten thousand dollars in the bank. This is lunacy!"

I said nothing. I didn't see anything either--even though my eyes were trained straight ahead, above dozens of heads, toward the front of the plane.

Elaina dropped her head, rotated it slowly a few times and sighed. With her glistening black hair now draping both sides of her face, she assessed the plain gold band that had been on her finger for thirty-three years. Then she slowly turned to me.

"No, Tom," she said, "I *insist* we talk about it now. I have to talk about it now."

"Elaina, please...don't start threatening to leave me again. You know that's something neither of us has ever done, no matter how angry we might have gotten. We've always cared too much for each other to talk such nonsense."

Taking her small hand in mine, we assessed each other's eyes. We both saw deep concern, but I saw something else. I saw she was dead serious, and I certainly didn't like it. Elaina and I had always seen eye-to-eye on almost everything.

Then, suddenly, we both jerked our gazes away. She pulled her hand from mine. We both grabbed our armrests, and I said, "Holy shit!"

The plane had dropped what seemed like twenty feet in a fraction of a second. The aluminum airliner bucked and shimmied, kicked and bounced violently. It was like riding in the belly of a huge, airborne, rodeo bronco. Passengers gasped. A few yelped. There was as much concern in Elaina's face and eyes as there was in mine. Had our seatbelts not been buckled, everybody onboard would have bounced off the ceiling or worse.

A few seconds and more than a hundred panicky thoughts later, the pilot righted the aircraft. Immediately the captain announced that everything was fine, they had just hit an air pocket. I reached for a cigarette but forced myself to dismiss the idea. The fuselage had filled with hyper-nervous chatter as heads snapped in various directions. It was a long few minutes before everybody finally settled down.

Elaina pulled the collar of her burgundy turtleneck away from her throat as if it would help her breath easier. She let out a deep breath, turned to me while I scoured the ocean far below and said, "Look at me, Tom. I've got to ask you something."

"Yeah, sorry, I was just thinking about something."

"I know, but it didn't happen. We're still up here, thank God."

Then she changed the tone of her whisper and demanded, "Tell me right here and now, what do you plan on doing with the award money? That's it, I want to know."

"Look, hon. You know what I want to do with it. We can hold on to a little more this time, if you want, but I'm giving it to people who need it more than we do, Habitat for Humanity."

Her face winced, as if I'd rammed a hardened steel blade into her breast and twisted it.

"You just don't care enough about us anymore, do you, about *me*?" She pulled her eyes from me, clasped her hands behind her neck, rolled her eyes to the overhead luggage rack and said, "I'm leaving you, Tom, tomorrow. You can stay in our rundown apartment while you build homes for total strangers, but I'm getting out. You've turned your back on me once too often."

"How can you say that? What's happened to you? What's happened to the Elaina who marched with me in D.C. all those times? Where's the girl, the woman, who demonstrated at Columbia and all those other schools? Where's the willful person who vowed at Woodstock to fight to her death against an unjust establishment? Geez," I paused for a moment, bobbing my head ever so slightly. Then looking around to be sure nobody could hear I said, "Look, hon, we *cannot* talk about this now. It's absolutely crazy to be whispering away our marriage up here in a plane full of people. Please, let's wait till we get home."

"OK, Tom, I'll wait, but we're going to resolve this as soon as we get there, one way or another."

Elaina then reached for the Newsweek, and I slumped into deep thought.

At first I tried to imagine how life would be without my soul-mate. All I could muster was fragmental thoughts, and I did not like them. With all the excitement the past few days, and the jetting back and forth, I couldn't seem to hold onto any one thought long enough to complete it. I knew Elaina had a point about making us more financially stable, yet I knew I'd feel guilty if I didn't allot most of the prize money and future royalties to needier causes. Such a gesture may seem irrational to most folks, I realize that. But the roots of my beliefs had been imbedded in my brain and soul a long time ago. As we continued to soar five miles above the Atlantic, I thought of just a few of the reasons why I'm so adamant about those beliefs.

While growing up, I walked the hardship walk. My family had very little. We knew all too well what it's like to do without. My father, Frank Soles, worked as an elevator operator in Manhattan. My mom, Estelle, stayed home, raised me and my brother Stanley, and read an awful lot of Silver Screen and Photoplay magazines. I think she often wished, and sometimes imagined, she was Elizabeth Taylor.

Neither of my parents relished sticking around any one place too long. They moved us all over Queens like four carnival roustabouts. By the time I hit fourteen (and began insisting I be called Tom not Tommy), I'd lived in eight different apartments--each one dingier than the last. By the time I'd entered the eighth grade, I'd already taken up space in seven different public schools. Of course, my brother and I had trouble in every one of them.

Being the new kid in school every year was bad enough, but we had other problems. First of all, Stanley and I always wore hand-me-downs, courtesy of our cousins. Try going to a new school or even a familiar one with outdated, oversized clothes and shoes so big you need to stuff yesterday's newspaper into the toes to keep them on your feet. The fact that Stanley was the studious type didn't help us win any popularity contests either. Two years my senior, Stanislaus, as I affectionately called him, was your basic, run-of-the-mill bookworm. Kids made fun of the braces on his teeth (I have no clue how they were paid for), often saying there was more steel in his mouth than there was in the Brooklyn Bridge. He wore Coke-bottle glasses complete with a Band-Aid on the nose rest, and he had a frail body. Those ever-present books glued to his nose didn't help matters either.

A late bloomer who didn't shoot up until sophomore year in high school, I was not only skinny, but short for my age as well. But that never stood in my way. Born with an extremely low tolerance for injustice and unfairness, I would go up against any kid, no matter what their size, if I caught them being mean to my big brother.

One time in third grade, I walked into the asphalt schoolyard across from our apartment building with my usual hopes of getting a game of stickball going. Armed with a pink rubber ball and broomstick bat, I saw some sixth graders gathered over a grating, outside the gymnasium wall. These were the tough kids, the ones who always wore black jeans and white shirts. They were flicking ashes from their Marlboros and looking down into the metal grating beneath their feet.

I went over to investigate, and when I looked into the steel grid below, there was Sylvester, cringing, covering his face, trying not to cry. The big kids were all spitting and dropping ashes on him. This future Nobel Laureate went absolutely nutso. I charged the heartless bullies, swinging the broomstick like a madman. I clipped a few pretty good before they knew what was happening, and when they scattered, the last one left was the biggest. A full head taller than me, smirking at me as if I were some kind of joke, I cracked the kid a good one over the head. The broomstick broke, the bully lost his smile, and I chased the bawling kid out of the schoolyard with what was left of the bat. For the rest of that year, nobody in school gave Stanley a bad time. Unfortunately, my parents moved us to another neighborhood the following summer and the same old troubles cropped up all over again.

By junior year in high school, I had devolved into someone else. Our family had lived in the same apartment for a record two-and-a-half years. Six feet even by now, still very thin, I was a first-string guard on Flushing High's basketball team. For the first time ever, I had plenty of friends. But things at home certainly hadn't changed much. My mother still shopped on Fridays, still for the same old TV dinners and cold cuts. And as always, by the time Tuesday rolled around, if Stanley or I wanted a snack, all that would be left was a half empty mayonnaise jar and a loaf of white bread. Stanley handled it, but I did not. Sick to the gills of always being broke, I did some things I'll regret for the rest of my life.

I'd lucked into a part time job at Saint Theresa's church rectory, working Monday and Thursday nights, but a dollar-fifteen an hour only netted me around eight dollars a week. That was enough to take a girl to the Keith's RKO movie theater, and maybe spring for pizza and Cokes afterwards, but that was about it. My friends fared much better. They always had plenty of "jingle," even though their families weren't much better off than mine. Instead of getting jobs they were always hustling and heisting.

Before I knew what hit me, I found myself compromising my staunch values. I started stealing--five dollars at a pop. When parishioners at Saint Theresa's came to the rectory to buy Mass cards, I'd pocket the stipend. Since I only worked eight hours a week, there were times when I didn't get the opportunity

23

to steal anything. That's when I found myself joining my friends on their money making escapades. As cool as they thought the easy money was, I always kept my feelings inside.

What I hated most was stealing donation canisters from store counters--taking considerable amounts of change and bills intended for kids with muscular dystrophy, polio or some other horrible disease. I didn't enjoy robbing crates of empty bottles from the back doors of bars and restaurants either, but the deposit money added up. I knew the guys and I had stepped well beyond the realm of serious mischief when we progressed to stealing girls' purses and wallets. This we would do at local dances or, in the summertime, at Rockaway Beach.

I detested myself for all of it, but tainted or not, I liked the unfamiliar feeling of money in my pockets. When I was very young and the ice cream truck came down the avenue there'd been far too many times when I was the only kid who did without. Then there were all those mayonnaise sandwiches, and a hundred other reasons for taking what didn't belong to me. But the madness suddenly stopped about two years after it started.

It was late at night and virtually no one was on the streets. I was walking home with a friend of mine, Billy Shea, after sneaking into a college beer-racket. We'd gotten thrown out for fighting, but our bellies were still filled with beer. A tight chain of closely parked cars buffered one side of the sidewalk and wall-to-wall, towering apartment buildings lined the other. Billy, having the malicious streak he did, was wrenching every car antenna he passed, breaking them at their bases. I told him how "fucked up" that was, but he wouldn't stop. That is until he spotted a very frail, very old lady one streetlight ahead of us.

"C'mon,' he said, picking up his pace, 'let's catch up to her."

"Whoooa," I said, "What the hell have you got up your sleeve, Shea?"

It wasn't until we were two steps behind the tiny, defenseless woman that Billy whispered, "I'm gonna snatch her purse, man."

I told him he'd better not dare try something like that, but Shea said it was easy money and he was doing it whether I liked it or not. With that, he grabbed the purse and started to run. But there were two problems. One, the woman must have sensed what was about to take place because, tiny as she was, she would not let go of that purse. Number two, the strap was a metal chain that was very tough to break. Billy dragged the screaming woman in the darkness. She slid face first on the cement sidewalk for probably fifteen feet before the chain broke.

Having no other choice I beat heels with him around the next corner and ducked into the basement of an apartment building. Minutes later three police sirens shrilled past the basement's small windows. I watched their red lights strobe across Billy Shea's maniacal face as he happily fished his booty from the purse. I was eighteen, and that was the last time I'd ever be involved in a theft.

Thanks to a strong tailwind, Flight 1402 touched down at Kennedy eight minutes ahead of schedule. When we disembarked shortly after, Elaina and I still weren't saying much. But that quickly changed when we reached the end of the exit ramp and stepped inside the terminal.

"Oh my god, Tom," Elaina said as she surprisingly grabbed my hand. "Look at all those reporters over there."

Beyond all the rows of blue plastic chairs in the waiting area were dozens of press people; CNN, ABC, CBC, MSNBC, and all the rest.

"Oh shit, I didn't want to go through this now," I said.

"Just be careful what you say," Elaina came back, "half the world will be seeing what takes place here. Don't lose your temper."

"Yeah, yeah, ye ..."

"That's him! There they are!" one of the press corps shouted. Then, as if on cue, all the cameras started rolling and clicking simultaneously. So did the questions.

"Mister Soles," the heavyset guy who first spotted us shouted above everybody else, "with your humble background, how does it feel to be a million dollars richer?"

"Not a whole lot different than it did the first time. By the way, do you do background checks on the side?"

Elaina tightened her small grip on my hand.

The entire assemblage chuckled from the remark, but the reporter fired right back, "What do you plan on doing with the money this time?"

"Don't tell me you're into financial planning too." There was another round of hearty laughs before I added, "It will be put to good use, I assure you."

A tall, handsome, blonde woman with spectacles, a necktie and a no BS demeanor asked, "I don't know if you've heard yet, Mister Soles, but a major book retailer here in the U.S. announced just hours ago that they are going to take your book off their shelves. Does that bother you?"

"No I haven't heard, being so busy and all. But yes, of course that bothers me. It also doesn't surprise me."

"Why doesn't that surprise you?" someone from the back of the still clicking, filming mob shouted.

"Have you yet read *Enough is Enough*, my friend? If you have, you know darned well there are some people in high places who are going to resent the truth."

"Mrs. Soles," a very familiar female face in the media world began, "do you support your husband's mission one hundred percent? And by the way, you are a very pretty lady. You *must* like nice things--jewelry, clothes, cars. How do you feel about him giving so much to charitable organizations?"

Elaina's grip on my hand loosened a bit, I felt my face heat up, but she said, "Yes, I'm behind him all the way. Now is not the time, and this isn't the place, for me to go into the pitfalls and evils of the present distribution of wealth in this country, which as you all know is the basis of his book. But I'll say this; Tom's beliefs should be irrefutable to anybody who is fair-minded, anybody who is capable of a rational, untainted thought process. Every worker in this country, and all others, *should* be

26

paid enough to take care of themselves and their families before any corporate profits are taken. He is on the right..."

"Excuse me, Elaina," I then said while hitching up my blue jeans a bit, "let me interject one thing. Do any of you people here, in this room, think it's perfectly fine that corporations raise prices and take larger and larger profits every year while their workers have their incomes and paltry benefits frozen or cut? Is it not sacrilegious that the huge majority of mothers in this country are forced to abandon their babies--their own flesh and blood--in daycare, because their husbands are no longer paid a livable wage? Should big shareholders who have more money than should be legal--shareholders who couldn't possibly spend their fortunes in thirty lifetimes no matter how hard they tried-- get much, much more while the people who work for them can't afford to fix the holes in their teeth?"

When the next newsman shouted, "Well what do you think about...?" I waved him off saying, "That's all we have folks. Elaina and I are very tired. We need to get home."

"But Mrs. Soles," the lady who asked the last question shouted above the now mumbling crowd, "you haven't answered the second part of my question. How do you feel about your husband giving away most of the money?"

"I can't answer that right now," Elaina said as we leaned our way through the media circus.

When we finally escaped and headed for the luggage carousel, one last question followed us across the shiny, bustling airport floor, "Although your book may not be fiction, some people are calling it a modern day *Grapes of Wrath*. Is that a fair assessment?"

With Elaina still in tow, and neither of us bothering to turn around, I raised a clenched fist high in the air, pumped it a few times, and said, "I'd sure like to think so."

During the cab ride home, Elaina and I didn't say much. The Middle Eastern driver, looking so stately in his clean white turban on the other side of the bullet-proof glass partition said nothing. For most of the trip, Elaina and I stared out our respective windows seeing little, enduring the gnawing tension hunkered in the back seat between us. Jet-lagged, exhausted, and uneasy, we both ruminated over our conversation on the plane. Silently, we watched the frenzied parkway traffic as if we were in trances.

The falling sun on this fine autumn Sunday afternoon splayed magical light on the towering oaks near Little Neck Bay. Their glowing leaves--gold, orange and crimson--lit up as if neon had replaced their lost chlorophyll. A jumbo jet low overhead roared as it descended toward the tarmac at nearby LaGuardia. Fifteen minutes from home now, Elaina finally said something, but I couldn't hear with the jet so close to the roof of the cab. When I asked her what she'd said, she just looked at me and slowly rotated her head. Seeing the sadness in her eyes tore at me, and it didn't let up after she looked back out the window. For the rest of the way home, I tried to think of an amiable compromise, and I came up with a few ideas. I would do almost anything to prevent my Elaina from leaving.

The funereal ambience continued until the cab turned onto Sampson Avenue. Checking the addresses, the driver slowly motored between the two interminable rows of apartment buildings. Block after block, so close and so tall, these towering brick piles stretched farther than the eye could see. Sometimes, particularly on overcast days, they seemed to lean in on both sides. God help any hapless claustrophobics who might stray here. Entering this shadowy, urban canyon would surely push them to the brink.

As the yellow cab skirted the endless chain of parked cars that eternally buffer the sidewalk here, Elaina pointed the driver toward our five-story walk-up. The oldest and smallest of all the pre-WWII buildings crowding the block, ours was halfway up on the right. Up and down the sidewalks, on both sides of the street, an entire army of multi-colored children were playing and horsing around. Afraid one of the small, international soldiers might dart out from between parked cars, the cabbie warily pushed forward. As he did, Elaina and I both noticed something peculiar.

A shiny black SUV, a big Lincoln Navigator, was double-parked in front of our five-story walk-up. Seeing such a vehicle in our neighborhood was quite an oddity, seeing one stopped was stranger yet. Then a tall, well-dressed man emerged from one of the glass and steel entry doors. Like a nervous owl, he glanced quickly to the right, and then to his left. As soon as he noticed our cab coming, he beat heels from the building as if it was engulfed in flames. He hurled himself into an open door of the waiting Lexus, and it sped off before he could even close it.

"Did you see that?" I asked Elaina.

"Yeeeaaahhh, that was weird. What do you suppose he...?"

"I don't know," I interrupted, "but he was up to something. I couldn't make out his face, could you?"

"No, the only thing I could tell was he was white, middle-aged, had gray hair, and was carrying something dark. Some kind of bag, I think."

"That's about all I saw, too. It looked like an oversized gym bag. And the way it flopped around when he started running it seemed empty."

"Oh well," Elaina said as the cab came to a stop. "Let's just get our luggage and get upstairs. This has been one hell of a day."

After paying and thanking the driver, I climbed out. But before retreating to the trunk for our luggage, I froze for a moment. Still standing in the street, the wind lifting my hair, I pointed at our building and said, "Look, honey! Look what the neighbors went and did."

"Was that sweet or what?" Elaina said, as she studied the broad white banner draped above the entryway. In large red letters it read, "WAY TO GO, TOMMY! WE'RE ALL SO VERY PROUD OF YOU!"

In other parts of the country, things may be different, but in New York neighborhoods such as ours, reverting to the adolescent version of one's name was, and still is, a compliment. Calling me, a fifty-nine year-old man, Tommy instead of Tom or Thomas, was a flattering, familial display of endearment by our friends. Titles, designations, even the Nobel Prize had nothing to do with acceptance or gaining respect on Sampson Avenue. All that counted was how you treated your fellow human beings. I'm honored that all my friends and neighbors always knew me as Tommy. Whoops, I almost forgot. Everybody didn't call me Tommy. There were a few exceptions. After *Enough is Enough* was first published, a few of the local teenagers started calling me "The Professor." That, too, was a pat on the back.

After slamming the trunk shut, Elaina and I hauled the luggage toward the front door. As we skirted three little girls and their hopscotch game, Manny Ruiz, the building's superintendent, came out. With his usual after-duty can of Budweiser in one hand, he held the door open with his other for old Mrs. Jacoby, the matriarch of "The Sampson Arms." Mrs. J had lived three–fourths of her eighty-one years there, and everyone, young and old, treated her with the utmost respect. But that by no means made her a stuffed shirt.

Leaning on her cane with one hand, patting my back with the other, she said, "Way to go, Tommy Boy. I've been following you for three days on the TV." Shifting her eyes to Elaina, a wide smile still on her face, she said, "Both of you looked beautiful in Stockholm, and at the airport."

Pumping my hand now with his free one, Manny added, "You sure did. And let me tell you, both you guys really gave it to dem reporters at the airport. You told 'em like it is. Man…everybody is so proud of you."

A few minutes later, Manny helped us schlep our suitcases up the five flights. Then, at long last, we were finally alone.

The first thing I did was go to the refrigerator for a glass of cold water. When I opened the insulated door, and saw what was inside, my heart suddenly felt like it was too large for my chest. It raced and it caromed off my ribs like a crazed elephant in a phone booth. Hot adrenaline seared every vein and capillary in my body. Immediately, a shroud of unfathomable dark doom took hold of my psyche, and I knew then and there it would never let go. In the course of one second I had entered a new world--an eerie, ominous, dark place that nobody should ever have to inhabit.

Heaped in front of me, on a glass shelf, were eight dead kittens. All of them with their throats slit. A note scrawled in their blood lay on top of them. It said, "You've only got one life left, Soles. If you want to keep it, stop the presses."

I reached in and felt one of the kittens. It was still warm.

Then there was a scream, Elaina's scream.

With my history of high blood pressure, I thought for sure my heart would implode. Totally submersed in fear, that previous sense of doom now insignificant, I rushed toward the bedroom in a state of unmitigated confusion. I was living out a macabre dream, so horrifying, so chaotic, it dizzied me.

I burst through the living room, up the short hallway, and swerved left into the bedroom. Once inside, I stopped short as if I'd hit a tempered glass wall. I stumbled two quick steps back as if I'd bounced off it. Elaina was hysterical. Hands over her eyes, her drooping head shaking a long procession of no's all she kept saying was, "Oh God, oh god, oh god, oh god..."

Strewn before us, on our bed, were thirteen blood-soaked copies of *Enough is Enough*. Every last page had been ripped out of them and scattered around the room. They were all over the carpeted floor, on the bureau, the dresser, and the night stands. Blood was all over everything. As if it had been sprayed with a water gun or a similar device, it dripped red on the walls, pictures, closet doors, window, and ceiling.

Chapter 5

For the next five days and nights, Elaina and I stayed at a hotel near LaGuardia Airport. Naturally, the detectives from the 109th precinct cordoned off our apartment and declared it a crime scene. They fine-combed every inch of it, as well as the building's common areas. They also checked out the street where the black SUV had parked, and questioned most of the neighbors, including the children who'd been playing out front. But they didn't find a single clue. Of course, they contacted the DMV, but with more than 6,000 black Lincoln Navigators in the city, there wasn't much to go on. Whoever committed this abominable crime knew exactly what they were doing. What concerned me most at this point was what they might do next.

Holed up in that hotel the way we were, Elaina and I felt like two hunted fugitives on the verge of being gunned down. Other than picking up our meals in the downstairs restaurant, we didn't step out of our room once. As for sleeping, *one can only* imagine how difficult that was. Take it from me; it's not easy when there's a steady stream of fear and heinous thoughts charging in and out of your mind. Occasionally, we'd hear a late-night cough, voice, or noise in the adjoining rooms or out in the hallway. Every time we did, we'd jolt upright in the bed. Horrible as the whole scenario was, hard as it was to get any sleep, being just a quarter-mile from one of the country's busiest airports didn't help either.

To call this experience trying would be the equivalent of calling Armageddon a skirmish. The world as we had known it had become a different place. We had no idea what to do. We hadn't a clue what was in store for us or where our lives were heading. I started growing a mustache and full beard. I had no plans to cut my hair for a very long time, either. Elaina cut her hair in the motel room, and it broke both our hearts.

Living in such sheer terror, neither of us even mentioned the money issue until our last night in the hotel. We were sitting in two straight backed chairs, at a table by the curtained window.

I'd just killed the TV after Jeopardy ended and was sipping a beer. Elaina fiddled with her glass of Sangria, looked into it and said, "You already know, Tom…I'm not going to leave you, don't you?"

"All we have is each other, hon. I, for one, know I wouldn't want to go on without you. I also know you feel the same way. Like I said on the plane, we have loved each other too hard and for too long to ever consider such a…look, I don't know, maybe you *would* be better off leaving me, Elaina. I'm afraid with what's happened. I'm scared shitless, and I don't want whoever's after me to get at you."

Waving me off now, she crinkled her forehead, and those sleek, dark-chocolate eyes grew adamant. As if it was a reprimand, she said, "Sure, we're scared. We've been talking about this, living this for almost a week now. But we don't know for sure if this nut case or those with him would really kill you or me. Heck no, it doesn't make me feel a whole lot safer, there are no guarantees, but even that policeman, Captain Geiger, said it could just be a threat. He had a point. If they wanted to get you they could have easily done so. Like it or not, Tom, I am not going through life without the man I love."

Though it had by then felt alien, a broad smile found its way to my face and I said, "You, young lady, are one tough cookie. I love you, you know."

"Oh stop. Don't go getting all mushy on me now."

"Listen, I've been thinking about the money thing. I'm ready to compromise…and I have a plan. Want to hear it?"

"Go ahead," she said, slowly lifting the wine glass to her lips.

"OK, I know how much you love this room, hrmmph, but I also know how long you've dreamed of taking a road trip around the country. What do you say we buy one of those RV's, you know, a motor home, and take that dream trip?"

Her face now lighting up like a teenager's on prom night, she said, "I'd love to! I'd rather do that than anything in the world. I don't believe it. How…how are we going to do it? You insist on donating most of the money. I've got my job to consider, and then there's the apartment."

33

"As far as the money is concerned, there's all too good a chance that the "enough" we've always gotten by on is no longer enough to keep us alive. As we said the other day—we *can't* go back to the apartment. Not for a while, anyway. So I'm thinking…"

"Wait, wait," Elaina interrupted, "do you just want to let the apartment go? Just give it up and get another place when we come back?"

"Let me finish, I was getting to that. I say we plan on travelling for six months to a year. That's our safest option. While we're on the road we can think about what we want to do next. We'll keep the apartment. I'll call Manny and tell him we'll send him the rent every month. That's not a problem."

"That's going to cost."

"Once again, that's a necessity. I'm not going to just give up my home, unless we decide that's what we want to do."

Elaina let this sink in for a moment. I took a long sip of beer, lit a cigarette. Then she said, "OK, sure. That makes sense. I'll call Rhonda at work again; tell her I'm going to need a longer leave of absence than I thought."

"That's exactly what I was thinking. Alright…that takes care of the apartment and your job. As for the money, look at the huge resurgence in sales the book has experienced. Since the media announced I'd be getting the prize two months ago, sales have gone through the roof again."

"Yeah, and we've already agreed there's no way in hell we're going to take it off the market. That's a done deal."

"Right, like I said, I'll die before I'll do that. But let me get back to the money thing now. Between the royalties coming in the way they are, and what I've gotten for the Nobel, money is a non-issue. I can easily make the donation to Habitat for Humanity and still have far more than we need for the trip. Once we get back, and decide what we want to do, we'll set ourselves up, hopefully return to a normal life, and continue our philanthropy."

Elaina thought the plan was perfect, except for one small hitch. The only stipulation she insisted on was that after we come back, we keep fifty-thousand dollars in our bank account.

And it made sense. With neither of us getting any younger, it was time we had some kind of small nest egg. We had to have something to fall back on.

After agreeing on that, I called Avis at the airport and reserved a car. Elaina and I did not own an automobile. Living in Flushing for so many years like we had, with public transportation being so convenient, it had been a long time since we'd owned one. But thankfully we'd always renewed our driver's licenses. With the rental car already secured, we packed our belongings and considering the circumstances, went to bed in reasonably good spirits.

* * *

The only thing separating the hotel from LaGuardia was the Van Wyck Expressway. Under cover of darkness early the next morning, Elaina and I hustled across it via an overpass that brought us right into the airport. There we picked up a Ford Taurus. As it was so early and a Saturday, traffic was nearly nonexistent. We made excellent time heading toward New Jersey. We zipped right through Queens, Brooklyn, and Staten Island, entering "The Garden State" just as a fresh new sun glinted on the eastern horizon. Crossing that invisible state line under such a glorious dawn sky made us both feel as if we'd been reborn. As if we had a chance. We not only felt somewhat safer but a heightened sense of anonymity as well.

Nevertheless, we weren't about to let down our guard. I may have stopped checking the rearview mirror, but I was still damned glad I had the Glock .45 automatic I'd bought the previous year. Buying the pistol seemed like a necessary evil after sales of *Enough is Enough* skyrocketed and the response from the business world escalated from mere grumblings to a loud vicious growl. As much as we needed the gun now, I wasn't very happy when I had bought it. I'd broken a promise I once made to myself. A vow I swore to myself the day I left Viet Nam. I can remember as if it was last week, being on that "freedom bird," rising above the jungle and rice paddies, watching them shrink and swearing up and down I'd never touch another firearm. Unfortunately, circumstances sometimes dictate that we go back on our word.

The first stop on our itinerary was Cherry Hill, New Jersey. We had checked our laptop before leaving the hotel and found out that two large RV dealers were in that area. Both seemed to have large inventories, so we figured they would be good places to shop prices and maybe strike up a deal. Also, both dealerships were convenient since we were heading south to begin with. With winter not all that far off, which direction to go in had been an easy decision. If Elaina and I were being forced to hide out, or if we had to keep on running, we might as well do it where it's sunny and warm.

After exiting the Jersey Turnpike in Cherry Hill, we stopped at a McDonald's drive-thru, grabbed two coffees then drove the short distance to the first RV dealership. We got there fifteen minutes before they opened, so Elaina and I sat in the car sipping our coffee. Peering through the windshield and tall cyclone fence, we could not believe the number of travel trailers and motor homes on the lot.

"My God," Elaina said, "how will we ever know what to pick out? There must be two hundred of them in there."

"I don't know, but like I said, we should definitely buy a used one. We're only planning to keep it a year, tops. If we bought a new one, we'd lose a small fortune when the time comes to flip it. Plus, I'm sure there'll be a lot more wiggle room when we begin to negotiate the price."

"I agree. We need to look for one just a few years old with low mileage," Elaina said as she lifted her bottom off the seat so she could see into the visor mirror. Once she got high enough to see, she quickly finger-brushed her new pixie cut. As she fluffed the short black bangs, her face winced and her eyebrows furrowed. Looking at her now, both our spirits deflated. The fact that she'd been forced to cut off her long beautiful hair was a grim reminder of just how serious our situation was. Our happy respite was no longer so happy, but we knew we still had to move forward with our plan.

Right then a man dressed like a Wall Street banker--three-piece, pinstriped suit and all--slid the huge, wheeled gate open. I gulped the last of my coffee and drove into the lot.

Just a few minutes after we had begun wandering amongst the acres of RV's, the fashion plate from the gate approached us. He was a fast talker who, like your basic run-of-the-mill doctor, acted as if his presence was an overly-generous, selfless gift. Right from the get-go the guy rubbed me the wrong way. He tried to lead us around by our noses but soon learned that wasn't going to happen. He was tall like me, about six-two, but probably fifteen years younger. He had an athletic build, and his looks were as flawless as his outfit. Beneath a head of impeccable blonde hair, he had a handsome, yet smarmy face that always seemed too close to ours when he spoke. And did he like to talk. The biggest mistake any salesman can make is to not listen to his customer, and believe me this guy was tough to get through to.

As full of himself as he was, and as much as Elaina and I wanted to bolt out of there, he had one unit we thought was perfect. It was an eleven-year-old, thirty-foot, Class A motor home. Forget about the age, this Winnebago was cherry, and it only had 31,000 miles on the odometer. It looked a streamlined, dressed up miniature bus on the outside, and the inside made our apartment look like a depression-era flat. Supposedly, it only had one previous owner. Whether it did or it didn't, we could easily see it had been loved. On its huge, panoramic windshield they had a price of $18,999.

After looking around it, inside it, and under it, we went for a spin. It felt awfully strange sitting so high off the road as I steered the big wheel, but the unit ran beautifully.

I would have bought it on the spot. With the signals Elaina was sending me I knew she would have, too. But I wanted to check out that other dealer first. I also wanted to feel out our *new friend*, Ronald C. Kincaid, to see how flexible he was on the price. After telling him we wanted to look further (much to his obvious chagrin) I asked him what his best price would be. Of course, he tried to drag us into the office to "talk," but I let him know I wasn't yet ready for that charade. He said they might take $17,500, plus tax, prep fees, and this and that. When I told him we might be back in an hour or so to talk, instead of being hopeful that he might have a sale, he looked at us as if we'd just yanked a commission check out of his breast pocket. As much as his demeanor bothered the hell out of me, something else irked me even more. Twice, during his pushy sales pitch, he stopped midsentence, looked closely at my face, and asked, "Are you sure we've never met? You look *very* familiar."

Though we hated to, Elaina and I did go back to see Kincaid. The salesman at the second dealership had been a true gentleman and ever so helpful. He asked us all kinds of questions so he could help us choose a vehicle that would not only fit our needs but our budget as well. But as hard as we looked, we couldn't find anything we liked as much as the one at the first place.

After going round and round with Kincaid and his manager for what seemed like half the day, but in reality was only an hour, we finally agreed on a deal. After that, when Elaina had gone to the ladies room, the general manager told me that this had been the hardest time he'd ever had "giving away" an RV. I just smiled and handed him a deposit.

After that, Elaina and I drove right over to the local branch of our bank and withdrew the funds. Fortunately, we got there ten minutes before their noon Saturday closing time. Soon after that, with Elaina behind me in the rental car, I rolled our new home out of the lot. We'd paid only $15,000--*out the door!* That included tax, title, license plates the works. We not only got a fantastic price, but the manager ended up eating all of the dealership's standard, nonsensical fees because I absolutely would not pay them.

After returning the Taurus right there in Cherry Hill, Elaina hopped into the RV with me. We were absolutely ecstatic. As I drove away from the Avis lot she raced up and down our new home on wheels checking out every nook and cranny. She was like a little girl on an Easter egg hunt. She finally plopped into the plush, oversized passenger seat next to me just as I steered the behemoth back onto the Jersey Turnpike. Sitting high, high above the road, all smiles, we felt as if we were perched on top of the world and it was rotating beneath us.

For the time being at least, all our happiness and excitement seemed to shrink our fears again. I can't describe with words how good it made me feel to see Elaina so excited and at ease after what we'd been through. I knew well and good we should savor this relief from our newly imposed mental bondage. I wanted to taste it, chew it slowly; make it last before digesting it. But something new was gnawing at me now. Something I wasn't going to bring up and let ruin all our well-deserved joy.

I did not like the idea that after Elaina and I had signed the paperwork, and she'd left me alone with Kincaid and the GM, Kincaid managed to put my name and face together. He'd finally realized who I was, and I did not like it one bit. Bad enough he knew the make, model, year, and color of the RV we would be driving, but there was even more. I had no choice but to also give him our cell number. He needed it so that when the permanent license plates arrived from New York he could call us and forward them to wherever we might be staying. I realized I just might be letting my imagination get out of hand. That the odds were huge nothing would ever become of this. But just the same, I did not like that guy. And with our lives possibly in very real danger, I didn't like having any bases uncovered. As much as that scenario with Kincaid and his boss bothered me, I decided not to tell Elaina about it. She already had enough on her mind.

After driving only sixty miles or so, I asked Elaina if she wanted to stop and find a campground. We hadn't gone far, but it was already crowding four in the afternoon. We'd gotten up very early that morning, accomplished a lot, and were beginning to tire. Driving the RV had been a barrel of fun, but being new at it demanded constant vigilance. I also figured we'd be much better off driving through Baltimore and D.C. early the next day; a Sunday morning. Lord knows we had nothing but time. Well, at least that's what we thought.

We exited I-95 in a very nice Maryland town called Aberdeen. We needed some supplies and there were all kinds of shopping right there near the interstate. All the big chain-stores were well represented in this squeaky-clean business district, but we really hoped to find a mom and pop place. We didn't have any luck, but we did manage to find one small supermarket with an unfamiliar name. And after parking the big rig in the far corner of the lot, we went in to buy groceries, beer, wine, and ice. The ice was a must since the fridge hadn't been plugged in yet and would take hours to get cold after we hooked up at a campground.

Surprisingly, the store had a fairly good selection of ball caps in one of its aisles. Believing that hats just might add another small degree of anonymity to our appearance, we each bought one. Elaina and I had to search for a few minutes, but we managed to find a couple that didn't have corporate or team logos on them. We wouldn't have cared if the store was giving them away, neither of us would ever allow ourselves to become walking billboards for some corporation, or a billionaire-owned sports team.

As soon as we got back to the camper, we removed the tags from our new caps, and put them on immediately. Elaina looked adorable the way she tipped the bill up on her burgundy one, and I told her exactly that. With a contented smile still on those full lips of hers, she said I looked real outdoorsy in my brown version. No matter how good, bad or indifferent they may have looked, we made a pact right there and then. Neither of us would ever take them off in public.

We spent that night in our camper parked in the back of a Cracker Barrel restaurant. Being new RVers, we hadn't a clue that most campgrounds as far north as we were had already closed for the winter. Nevertheless, after storing all the food and ice and having a couple of drinks and dinner, we cuddled up in the back bedroom and slept like two sleep-deprived infants. The next morning, feeling all rested, chipper and cozy in our new home, we decided not to shoot straight to Florida. There certainly was no reason to rush. Neither of us had ever seen the Great Smoky Mountains in Western North Carolina, and now that we had the opportunity, we figured why not. It was still autumn and maybe not too late to see the leaves turning up there.

Benign as our reasons were, the decision to go to the Smokies would soon turn out to be an unfathomable mistake.

Chapter 6

The morning of November 2nd was the fifth time we had woken up in the Winnebago. We were having a ball in it, and Elaina had the tiny kitchen all set up just the just way she wanted. It was our second day in the Asheville area, and the weather forecast promised another unseasonably-mild autumn day. Sitting at a picnic table outside the camper at first light, we were already working on our second cup of coffee. As the new dawn greeted the forest around us, illuminating a spectacle of scarlet and gold leaves, Elaina whispered so as not to disturb the other campers.

"Honey, what do you say we drive up to the Blue Ridge Parkway this morning? Everyone is saying that it's utterly gorgeous."

"Sure," I said, admiring the natural beauty all around us, "I guess it's safe."

"What's safe, Tom? We don't know how safe we are sitting right here. We can't just lie down and die. We're going to go right on enjoying ourselves. Yeah...sure, we still have to be vigilant, but that's it."

I pulled a Carlton from my pack, tapped the end of it on the wooden picnic table. You're right, honey, freak it, we're going to have an experience we'll never forget. By the way, we're going to have to buy one of those little cameras. What do they call them...digital?"

"Yesss," she said raising her brows in an exaggerated fashion, going popeyed on me. "And guess who's going to end up figuring how to work the thing."

"All right, all right, quit picking on me. So what if I'm a bit, what do they call it today, electronically challenged?"

"I'd like to get one today...hey, do you hear that? Shhhh, listen."

From somewhere just behind the tree line came a loud knock-knock-knock as if someone was banging one of the tree trunks with an undersized hammer.

"Yeaaah, I hear it. It sounds like…"

"Look Tom," Elaina interrupted, "There it is. See it."

Flying from the bough of a tall pine tree, with the sun's first soft rays setting it aglow, was the largest woodpecker we'd ever seen. A full foot and a half in length, it looked a little goofy, yet majestic, at the same time. It had a tall red crest atop its head and a white line running down its blackish neck. As it flew right above us, it called out as if it was scolding us. A loud, irregular kik-kikkik-kik-kik resonated throughout the campground and woods.

* * *

About an hour later, on the way to the Blue Ridge Parkway, we made a quick stop at a Wal-Mart. For the first time in as long as I can remember, we splurged. For many years we'd been splitting paper towels in half, cutting out grocery coupons, buying day-old bread. This day we sprung for that camera, and two reasonably-priced pairs of binoculars. On the way to the checkout, Elaina spotted *A Field Guide to the Birds East of the Rockies,* which we also bought. Minutes later, as I drove to the parkway, she checked the guide and found out the bird we'd seen was a Pileated Woodpecker.

The views from the Blue Ridge were absolutely breathtaking on that fall morning. Beyond every twist and turn, the panoramic visions of the Great Smoky Mountains were nothing short of astounding. Guaranteed, anyone who visits this place will leave with full color, mental snapshots indelibly forged in their mind. Folds of smooth rolling mountains stretch out in seemingly endless rows, in every direction, for as far as one can see. Mystical blue "smoke" rising from the countless peaks only intensified the magnificence surrounding us. Elaina and I just had to pull over to a small parking area and get out of the camper.

"Look at this, Tom," she said in awe, "look at the colors. It's like a red, orange, and gold quilt has been spread over every inch of these mountains. This is unbelievable."

She took some photographs with the new camera, and then we just stood there for a few moments. Neither of us said a word. It was as if being in the midst of such beauty, we were partaking in a religious experience. Eventually, though, Elaina broke the silence. She'd noticed a nature trail leading down into the woods.

"Hey," she said, "let's take a walk. C'mon, Tom."

"I don't know. You sure you want to?"

"Oh, don't be an old poop, let's go!" she said, brimming with excitement.

With the new binoculars hanging from our necks, I said, "Shit yes, what the hell."

I locked the Winnebago, and we carefully walked down a steep incline leading into the trees.

Happy as a teenager on prom night, she slung her arm around my waist as we entered the woods, and I did the same to her. Looking up into my eyes she squeezed my side and said, "We're going to have one hell of a time on this trip, Tom. Can you imagine what it's going to be like in Colorado and Montana this spring? What it's going to be like in..."

The shot came from a high-powered rifle. There was no warning. Coming from the trees in front of us, the ear-splitting blast sounded like it was about fifty yards away. A cold chill froze my spine, and for just a splinter of that second, shock and confusion numbed my brain.

With my arm still around her waist, I felt Elaina jolt backwards. Reflexively, I tightened my grip on her and stiffened my arm, but it did no good. I could not stop her. My wife, my soul mate, my confidante, my life, lifted into the air and flew six feet backwards.

Time stood still. *Oh my good God in heaven*, I thought, *this can't be happening*. But it was, and Elaina went down, back first, on the dusty trail. I saw her head bounce off the dirt and snap forward. Her burgundy cap flew off and blood of the same color was all over the front of her white sweatshirt. Yanking my head back around I screamed into the woods, "Nooooo, you mother fuckerrr!!! Come get me! Come get me now you fucking animal!"

Then I spun around, took two steps back, and fell knees to the ground alongside Elaina. As I held her in my arms, her cheek next to mine, I heard rustling leaves and snapping branches. I didn't know if the shooter was heading towards me or taking off in the opposite direction. I hoped he was coming for me. Holding her by the back of her head, feeling the dirt in her short hair, my wife took her last shallow breaths.

"Elaina, Elaina, nooo, please God nooo," I pleaded.

But in a matter of seconds, the inevitable moment arrived. Just before it did, Elaina spoke her last words. No, she whispered them, just four words. So weak were they that, had we not still been cheek to cheek, I would never have heard them. As she left to meet her maker, she said, "Tom...please...be careful." Warm tears then coursed my cheeks and dripped onto Elaina's. As I wept her body shuddered and quivered with mine.

Then, not a moment too soon, I spoke softly in her ear. "Don't worry, honey, you won't be alone for long. I promise, I'll come to get you."

I don't know how long I laid there holding my Elaina, but I stayed with her on that mountain trail long after her body went cold. I can't come close to explaining the feeling of desolation and mental agony that overcame me. The thoughts that crowded my consciousness were filled with hate and revenge, uncommon love and monumental loss.

For the longest time, I thought I'd never get up. But eventually, I did. About the time the sun was directly above us, I rose to my knees and gently rested Elaina's head on the red Carolina soil. I picked up her cap and trudged up the incline toward the camper. With old tears and new tears clouding my vision and my equilibrium out of kilter, I kept slipping, falling, and sliding face first in the dirt. I don't know if it happened three times or four, but I do know that each time I went down, I stayed there a while. Each time, I pounded my fists into the ground with what little strength I had left. I also cried--I wailed like a horrified man being led to the gallows.

When I finally reached the camper, I called the authorities on Elaina's cell phone. Unfamiliar with the phone, shaking like I was, it took several efforts to dial 911 on the tiny keys. A short time later, the National Park Rangers arrived. The police and ambulance were not far behind.

The law officers told me right off that Elaina's death had all the ingredients of a typical, careless hunting accident. After investigating the scene for two days, they said they hadn't found a single meaningful clue, not even the spent shell. Of course, when the autopsy was performed they did find the bullet in my sweetheart's chest. I don't remember what caliber it was, but they said it was the one most widely used by deer hunters. They also said whoever pulled that trigger must have mistaken Elaina's white sweatshirt for the tail of a deer.

The ironic part of this horrendous tragedy is that, if the mindless fucking cretin who ended my wife's life *was a hunter*, he was also a poacher. Deer season in Western North Carolina hadn't begun yet. It was still three weeks away. On top of that, the area around the Blue Ridge Parkway is a wildlife preserve, and hunting of any kind, at any time, is illegal. Although I'm fairly certain the investigators were correct in declaring Elaina's death a hunting accident, I will carry to my grave a small gnawing doubt.

Since I was in no condition to drive, one of the police officers drove me and the RV back to the campground in Asheville. I stayed inside that camper for six straight days, most of the time curled up in bed. For a while I could still smell Elaina's lilac perfume in the blanket and sheets. Not certain whether the scent was deepening my grief or giving me some small sense of comfort, I kept myself wrapped up in them. When the familiar fragrance began to dissipate, I sprayed more of the purple liquid onto the bed. I did this several times.

I really had no right being alone in my condition, but I was, and I wanted to be. Other than my brother, his wife, and my mother (who lived with them) there was nobody to turn to, nowhere to go. When I phoned Stanley, he insisted I come back up to Long Island and stay with them for a while. But I wasn't about to endanger what was left of my family, and as I said before, all I wanted was to be left alone.

Since both Elaina's parents had died in an automobile accident twelve years earlier, and she'd been an only child, there was nobody to notify in her family. She did have two cousins and an aunt, but years before her own death Elaina's mother had a falling out with the aunt. Their small family had been estranged ever since. As for Elaina and I, we never had any children. She was unable to conceive. Although that had bothered us for many years, it now seemed like an extraordinary blessing. For there were no children to advise of their mother's death.

Chapter 7

Exactly one week after Elaina's passing, the RV's permanent license plates arrived. I thought about that sleazy salesman, Kincaid, but seriously doubted he had anything to do with what had taken place. I contemplated every possible scenario and decided the odds of him being involved, particularly so soon, were miniscule. Had I known for sure that he was involved, I would have gone right back to Jersey and ended him—no matter what the consequences.

After bolting on the plates in a pouring rain, I unhooked the camper, put the Glock in my glove compartment, cranked up the engine and pulled out of that campground. I'd lost a few pounds and still looked like hell, but it was time to move on--or at least try to. I hadn't discarded any of Elaina's belongings. I left her toothbrush alongside mine in the holder, her new potholders where she'd hung them and her makeup in its tray on her nightstand. On my own nightstand I left her burgundy cap. Every night before going to sleep I would kiss it, and to this very day, I still do.

Before heading out of Asheville, I had to make one stop in town. As much as I dreaded it, there is no force in this world or beyond that could have stopped me. I had to go to a crematory to pick up Elaina's remains. With all the sorrow, unhappiness, and fear for the future already weighing on every frayed nerve in my body, I didn't know if I could handle it. All I can tell you here is that I did pick up the brass urn with its four-pound contents. I did it as quickly as I could. As I paid and signed the necessary papers, I somehow managed to fight back the flood of dark, devastating emotions swelling inside me. But as soon as the business transaction was completed and I picked up that urn, I couldn't stand it anymore. I rushed for that door like a man on the verge of vomiting.

Stepping out of that building into the rain certainly didn't help. Clutching Elaina to my chest as if she'd just returned from the dead, running through puddles beneath that doomsday sky, all my pent up pain and misery imploded at once. I did not retch. Along with tears, I *spewed* those vile feelings all over the asphalt parking lot. Once inside the camper, with my head and convulsing shoulders dripping wet, I continued to purge the hurt. I didn't get rid of it all, of course. It should only be that easy. None of us are capable of ever completely shaking such an immense sense of loss. I cannot (here or anywhere else) expound any further on how I felt that day. What I've already described in these last two paragraphs is about as close to reliving that day as I ever want to get. I am sorry.

It was raining even harder when I pulled onto I-26-south. Due to a fast approaching cold front a posse of low, gray, burgeoning clouds had rushed in and packed tight in the sky. The wind blew with all the force of a gale, and the way the drab rain pelted my windshield was nothing short of an assault. The oversized wipers slapped back and forth so hard it was as if they were in a panic and wanted to break free. The gunmetal sky was so low, or Asheville so high, that those clouds seemed to buff the RV's roof as I drove. Visibility was so bad; some vehicles had pulled onto the highway's shoulder. But I was finally rolling, and I did not want to stop.

About two hours later, I pulled off the interstate in Columbia, South Carolina. I needed coffee more than I did gas but figured I'd do the two birds with one stone thing. After pumping just shy of half a tank, I tugged my brown cap real low on my forehead and hustled through the rain into the truck stop. By now my beard and mustache were almost fully-grown.

Once inside, I headed straight for the men's room. But I didn't quite make it. After making my way past the cashier and through the store section I continued down a long hallway. About halfway down, I passed the entrance to a truckers lounge and just happened to glance inside. Two steps later I stopped dead in my tracks. I backpedalled to the open doorway and took a second look inside. About fifteen truckers, slouched in blue plastic seats, were watching a wall-mounted television. And on the screen of that TV was a picture of Elaina. I only caught the tail-end of what the newscaster said.

"...when we return after these messages from our sponsors."

Standing out in the hallway, off to one side of the door, I pulled the bill of my cap lower yet. I raised the collar of my damp jacket and wished I'd had on my sunglasses. The succession of useless commercials seemed to last about fifteen minutes, though only two or three had ticked away. One promised a more exciting and sexier life if you bought their toothpaste. Another guaranteed their product would get rid of your acid reflux—even though there was a "highly unlikely chance" you could have about a dozen more serious side-effects. By the time all the nonsense ended, two more truckers had entered the room, one had left, and I had dropped my head all three times, pretending to look at my watch.

Finally the newsman with the high forehead and glasses returned, so did the picture of Elaina.

"As you first heard here last week, Elaina Soles, the wife of recent Nobel Prize recipient Thomas Soles, died in a suspected hunting accident while walking with her husband along a nature trail in Western North Carolina. This sad event took place mere days after she and Mr. Soles returned home from Stockholm to a horrific, bloody scene and a very disturbing death threat in their Queens, New York apartment.

There is now growing suspicion that these two events may be linked. Despite the findings of North Carolina authorities, many people around the country believe that both crimes may have been committed by what they call "corporate vigilantes." Many who've read Thomas Soles bestselling book, *Enough is Enough*, believe that since it vilifies Corporate America, some CEO's, and this country's elite, may be taking revenge. While it is true that a second major bookselling chain has taken Soles's controversial book off its shelves this week, at this point, there is no evidence of foul play.

But that's not holding back the rising tide of suspicion and discontent that stretches from New York to California. Seeing so many people taking to the streets is reminiscent of the tumultuous 1960's and 70's. On Friday, here in Manhattan, an estimated 15,000 protesters carrying signs and chanting, "enough is enough" showed up in front of the New York Stock Exchange. Yesterday, Chicago's Grant Park had a similar demonstration, and there are still others planned later this week for Boston, Detroit, Denver and L.A.

As always, we will keep you posted on any forthcoming developments in this story."

I just stood there, stupefied. I had no idea how people were reacting to our tragedy. Since returning from Sweden, I hadn't listened to, watched, or read any news at all. What I had just seen and heard stunned me. It gave me the chills. Throngs of goose-bumps tightened the flesh on both my arms. But at the same time, I also felt a warm, benevolent glow inside. Though I'm an interminable doubting Thomas, always having difficulty accepting the life after death thing, I had this uncanny feeling in that truck-stop hallway that Elaina had been standing there also. It was as if she'd been right there alongside me watching that news report.

I continued toward Florida as if the Winnebago was on auto-pilot. Sure, I braked, steered, and accelerated, but all that was instinctual. There were a host of more pressing thoughts tracking through my head, like countless boxcars on a runaway train. For the most part, they were of Elaina, but a few times that malicious snake--suicide, slithered through the dark recesses of my brain. How to do it? Where to do it? Should I do it? But there was an upside. While driving through the Carolinas and Georgia, that grievous temptation was popping up less and less often than it had during those six days in Asheville. I'm sure part of the reason was that I kept telling myself Elaina, if she could, would have booted me a good one--right in the ass--for entertaining such thoughts.

While motoring alongside endless stands of lofty green pines on I-95, there were times I wished Elaina *had* left me. If she had, just like she'd threatened on the way home from Stockholm, she'd still be alive. I still would have been on the run alone, as I was now. But each time that heartbreaking reality jabbed at me, I parried it away. I knew well and good that Elaina never would have left me. She loved me as much as I did her. She stayed with me because I was as big a part of her as she herself was. All she'd have wanted at this point is for me to go on living my life. That and to "be careful," as she said when she was dying in my arms.

Chapter 8

For the next three weeks, I bounced all over Florida. Rarely did I stay anywhere for more than one night. The only time I spoke to anyone was when it was absolutely necessary. Whether checking in or out at campgrounds, state parks, stores or gas stations, I was as brief as possible. I felt like a serial-killer on the run, like the scornful target of a nation-wide manhunt. I couldn't look anyone in the eye unless I had my sunglasses on. And don't forget, I was deep into one of the darkest states of mourning imaginable. I had to live with the senseless death, possibly murder, of someone who had been everything to me. People often wonder, do I love him or her--I just don't know for sure. For the sake of anybody in such a quandary, there is only one question you need to ask yourself— would I, unflinchingly, give my life to save theirs? Amen. That's it. I know what my answer would've been had I had the opportunity to save Elaina.

By the time I rolled into Key West, I was desperate for some human interaction. Beginning to think I'd rather risk being murdered than go on the way I had been, I hailed a cab minutes after checking into a campground. When I climbed into the back of the taxi (a gaudy pink one, by the way), the driver pointed to a small placard mounted on the dashboard. Considering my predicament, I thought its message was quite ironic.

So sorry, I cannot hear or speak.
Please write down your destination.
Thank you. Francis Drake--Bahamas

The old black man then handed me a pen and paper. I did as the sign said, passed the directions over the front seat, then leaned back and tried to relax.

It was an early December late afternoon, sunny with temperatures in the low eighties. The sidewalks along Duval

Street's bars, shops, and restaurants were as cluttered as Madison Avenue's during rush-hour. Tourists with bouncing belly-bags and flowery tropical shirts bustled along like a herd of disoriented Guernsey's. Mixed with them was your typical Key West cast—hucksters, hard-lucksters, dream chasers, law breakers, gays, pirates, fisherman, and sixties throwbacks.

By the time Francis Drake slowed down to let me out in front of Sloppy Joe's Bar, I was seriously questioning my decision to go there. I knew there'd be a lot of people around and figured I could handle it. But thinking about a place and being there are two different things. Since arriving in Florida I'd been camping in obscure parks; in places like Lake City, Cedar Key, Homosassa, and Belle Glade. Obviously the "Southernmost City" wasn't the best place for me to come out of hiding, but I was there, and I sure could use a cold beer.

I got out of the cab and quickly reintroduced my cap's bill to the top of my sunglasses. Head down, finger-combing the gray hair that now hid part of my ears, I zigged and zagged through the onslaught of humanity in front of Sloppy Joe's, then turned down the Greene Street side of the building. The place was jam-packed. Loud music from the open-air bar blared out onto the streets, drowning out all the raucous conversations inside. I kicked heels down the sidewalk, gladly leaving Duval Street's carnival-like atmosphere behind. I was a block away before the lyrics of Buffett's "Why Don't We Get Drunk and Screw" faded into background music. At that point my other senses kicked back in, and I was able to smell the creamy, fruity scent of all the front-yard gardenias and jasmine.

It felt so good stretching my legs after the long drive down from Jupiter that I didn't mind delaying that first cold beer. I made a left onto Whitehead Street and walked part of the way to Ernest Hemingway's house. Strolling alongside tight rows of the very same Conch houses that "Papa" himself had passed eighty years earlier was a nostalgic trip down history lane. This was the same route the twentieth-century's most influential author stumbled along so many times after his legendary drinking bouts. As I made my way up the narrow sidewalk, past the tiny front yards with all their palm trees and flowery tropical flora, it seemed ludicrous that I had been awarded the same prize for excellence as the man who single-handily revolutionized American literature. The way I saw it, I had about as much relevance in the literary world as a comma did in one of his novels.

A few blocks before Hem's house, I came upon a corner bar called Casablanca West. It, too, was of the open-air variety; and despite a smattering of towering bamboo shoots around the outside, I could plainly see all the customers inside. The place looked like an oasis to me, but still, I stepped tentatively under its thatched roof. With only a few empty stools here and there, I opted for one of two at the far right of the crowded M-shaped bar.

There was a cypress-planked wall behind me, and I liked it that way. Bob Seger's "Beautiful Loser" played on the Wurlitzer, as a row of beam-mounted ceiling fans rotated ever so lazily. When a frazzled blonde barmaid, wearing a tank top and too many tattoos, approached me, I sprung for a Corona light.

Alternating hits from a cigarette with sips of cold beer, I surveyed the chattering crowd for a few minutes. A hand-painted wooden sign behind the bar said, "NO SHOES, NO SHIRT, NO PROBLEM!" I blended in fine with my denim shorts and tee shirt, yet still felt uncomfortably conspicuous.

Turning my attention outside the bar, I saw a strange character chaining a bicycle to one of the bamboo shoots. Warm as it was, the slight man was actually dressed in a green army field jacket, black jeans, and high black boots. Though the stringy, oily hair brushing his shoulders was still black, he had the face of a man in his late seventies. I thought for sure he must be homeless.

Oh shit, I thought, *that would be just my luck. Watch this guy come right over here and try to hustle me for drinks.*

Sure as hell, he came inside, stood there a moment, gave the crowd a quick assessment then focused on me. From behind my dark glasses, I watched him out of the corner of my eye.

Ohhh Shit, here he comes!

Of course, he marched right over to the vacant stool beside me. As I drained what was left in my bottle, I could feel his stare on the side of my face. I wanted to ask him what the hell his problem was but just ignored him and kept my eyes on the barmaid. When she finally came to take his order, she leaned over the bar and presented this guy with her cheek.

He kissed it softly and said "Hello Crystal! How is my favorite girl today?"

Then, after a quick exchange of pleasantries, he said, "Give me a scotch and soda," then pointing at my empty bottle, "And give this gentleman another Corona."

I turned and looked at him and he said, "That is, if I may have the honor of having a drink with you."

I almost flipped backwards in my stool, not only because of the drink offer but also because of this scruffy old man's voice. It was absolutely eloquent. He had a Mediterranean accent that added an unusual richness to his words. The way he so meticulously spaced them with his authoritative voice immediately put me to mind of Old World royalty.

"Yeah, sure," I said, "I'll have another. Thank you very much."

He smiled, and his craggy face lit up. Then he extended his hand and said, "I am Arturo Giovanni, and I'm pleased to meet you."

"My name is Frank, Frank Delaney," I lied, as we shook hands and Crystal plunked down the drinks.

"May I call you Frank, Mister Delaney?"

"Sure, that would be fine."

He saluted me with his drink, I did the same, and we both took a swallow. Then he dug into one of the pouch-like pockets of his field jacket, as if searching for what he'd say next. When he extracted a new pack of imported cigarettes, he rapped it on the bar a few times and said, "How long have you been in town...Frank?"

"Just a few hours. I'm only staying a day or two, then I'll probably knock around the middle Keys for a while."

"Have you been to Key West before?"

I nodded my head, saying, "Yes, I've been here three times before...with, with my wife."

He nodded meditatively, as if evaluating what I'd just said then lit up a cigarette. He took a long, deep draw. Then, as he exhaled a slow steady stream of smoke toward the overhead fan, his eyes looked as if they were straining. When he turned back to me his face tightened up. A wave of deep concern washed over it, and the wrinkles on his forehead deepened. He took a slow cautious glance to both sides then said in a low voice, "I am so very sorry to hear about your wife, Mister Soles."

Excuse the expression, but I almost shit green. It was now my turn to look back and forth, but I did it quickly. Then, in a forceful whisper, I said, "Who the hell are you, Buddy? What are you talking about? You don't know me. I told you, my name is Delaney."

"I am an artist, Mister Soles. My work is known all over the world. I spend part of my time here in Key West and part in Milan, where I have a second home. In my profession, I deal with many different shapes. As a blind man compensates by attuning his remaining senses, I have developed over the years an uncanny eye for shapes. When I first saw you from the sidewalk I knew who you are by your facial features. But don't be overly concerned. With your mustache and beard, the glasses, and the hat, not many others would ever recognize you."

Looking deep into his dark eyes, I said, "I think maybe I should leave."

I reached for my cigarettes, and he gently laid his hand on my shoulder.

"I am so sorry. I did not mean to upset you. You are looking at one of your biggest admirers. I have read your book. I agree wholeheartedly with all of your convictions."

I then turned my eyes to the wooden bar. I let out a long breath then slowly rotated the ashtray in front of me. Continuing to fiddle with it I said, "You obviously know I've been on the run."

"Your dreadful misfortune has been all over the news-- worldwide. Have you not been watching it?"

"No, I haven't. I've been trying to handle my personal hell. I don't need any added distress. Look, I appreciate the beer, but I better get out of here."

"Mister Soles, I know what it is to fear for my life. I may not have anyone looking to do me harm, but I am an old man, and I have a disease that is gunning for me. I have leukemia, and it is going to kill me within six months."

The old man paused for a drag on his cigarette. Then, with a dreamy, nostalgic look in his eyes, he went on, "I also know what it is like to lose the woman you love. I have lost two very special women in my lifetime, and though I shall never get over them, the pain is no longer excruciating like yours must now be. I promise you, your agony will also lessen over time, Mister Soles."

I took a long gulp of my Corona. "Thank you Arturo. You're a kind man."

"Will you stay for another beer? I would truly like that."

"Sure, why not? But only if you'll let me pay this time."

And I did pay. For the first time, we both relaxed against the backrests of our stools. I fired up a smoke and he said, "*Enough is Enough,* what an appropriate title. I'll bet that has a...what do you call it...a double meaning?"

"You are very insightful, my friend. It..."

Arturo interrupted with an excited wave. "Wait, wait! Let me see if I was correct in my thinking. First, it means the unfair distribution of wealth in this country should no longer be tolerated. Secondly, that the richest two percent of Americans are unconscionable in their quest for yet more when the lifestyle of the masses is quickly devolving to that of a third-world country."

"Exactly! It boggles my mind that any human being with enough wealth to live hundreds of lifetimes could possibly be greedy enough to want even more. And mind you, at the expense of a grossly underpaid majority that is losing more and more every year. You tell me, how that can continue."

"Not only that, Thomas, but as you said in your book, what will it be like for most workers and their families ten years from now?"

I nodded, took a swallow of beer then said, "It's going to be disastrous. As you read in my book, if Corporate America keeps doing business as usual, you'll soon see many, many more people living under bridges. Listen, Arturo, I've been camping all over Florida for the past month, and you would be shocked by the number of people, and families, that are now living in beat-up travel trailers and broken-down RV's. And many of them have jobs!"

"Look," I went on, guiding both my palms forward in a slight, half-shove motion, "the bottom line is this. Those with disposable income put money into the stock market. The corporations they invest in are all hell-bent on getting them at least a fifteen, twenty percent return on their investment every year. OK, under the system we live in, that seems all well and good. But how do those companies make enough money to pay those dividends? They cut their workers benefits and sometimes their salaries. They shrink, for example, the cereal box. They fill it with less product. They raise the price, which is nothing short of manufactured inflation. This is the eleventh hour for the American working-class, Arturo. While they're being forced to cut back on medications, trips to the dentist, and every other conceivable necessity, those corporations are lining the pockets of the haves with yet more tainted dollars.

Please, forgive me for rambling. But once I get going on this subject I get all wound up. And I should, because despite all the other injustices eating at our society like insatiable tumors, the stock market is the most damaging. That and the lack of campaign finance reform--we can no longer allow the selling of what's left of our democracy to special interests. Whewww, that's it. I've had it, enough with the disastrous effects of greed for one sitting. What do you say we have one more drink? Then I've *got to* shove off."

I spoke with Arturo Giovanni for a while longer. He told me that although the demonstrations and marches had become less frequent, he'd recently seen a few cars with *Enough is Enough* bumper stickers on them. I hadn't as yet seen any, but just knowing it was so, allowed me a deep sense of achievement. Despite my enormous misfortune, my book was having a positive impact on people. I thanked Mr. Giovanni when I left and gave him my phone number. I couldn't help but to feel a strong affinity toward this man who I at first shunned. And I sincerely hoped he'd keep in touch with me during the final months of his life.

Arturo did call me—ten minutes after I left Casa Blanca West. I was in another cab, this time heading back to my camper. He said a man he didn't know had approached him right after I left. The stranger asked him if I was Thomas Soles. Possibly he was just another curious admirer with an unusual aptitude for shapes and no malicious intentions. Possibly he was not. Either way, thirty minutes after Arturo's call, I was following the camper's high beams across the dark, deserted islands north of Key West.

As I alluded earlier on, driving a thirty-foot motor home is more physically and mentally demanding than operating a car or an SUV; especially at night, especially after being up and about all day. But that didn't stop me. I wanted out of Key West and drove six hours into the Florida night.

For the first time since finding those poor slaughtered kittens in our refrigerator, I feared I was becoming delusional. Was I losing it--becoming a paranoiac? Was rushing off the way I just had, normal behavior for somebody in my predicament? Exactly what is "normal" behavior for a person living a hellish nightmare such as mine? Could I keep this up? Would my condition worsen? All these fears and more kept revolving through my mind as I smoked cigarettes, drank coffee, and pushed on.

Finally, around 1:00 AM, exhausted and mentally drained, I pulled into a Fort Pierce truck stop. Another mile would have been impossible. After killing the lights and ignition, I stumbled to the back of the camper, kissed Elaina's cap, and fell asleep before hitting the bed. I was now a considerable distance *north* of where I'd been the previous morning when I'd left *for* the Keys.

The next morning a brash chorus of hissing air-brakes and grumbling diesel engines had me up before dawn. I'd slept soundly but not nearly long enough. There was no way I could have--it sounded as if I was smack in the middle of a state-wide truckers' rally. On top of that, there were all the headlights. Continual flashes of harsh white beams lit up the bedroom like the blinding lightning bolts of a ferocious tropical storm. Exhausted as my body still was, my mind was already in high-gear. It picked right up where it left off just a few hours earlier.

The urge to push farther north was indisputable. Still wearing my sneakers and the same clothes I'd slept in, I ran inside for a coffee, ran back, cranked up the engine and followed the truckers and their million pound loads back onto I-95. I had no idea where I was going but knew damn well it had to be farther north.

The convoy soon left me behind on the dark deserted highway. Alone with just my thoughts I looked toward the eastern horizon. There I saw the first faint glow of light. It was every bit as pink as my bloodshot eyes.

Jesus, I thought, *why does it have to be this way? What did I do to deserve all this? All I did was write a book of truths. I wonder if they sought revenge on Orwell after 1984 came out. Did they try to enact it? Shit...nobody should have to live this hell. Where do I go next? What do I do? How long can I keep this up? Is it better to face the music; go back to New York; let the chips fall where they may? Should I just pull into the next rest stop and put the Glock to my head? I mean...what the fuck do I have to lose? If I don't, where will I be in a year, next month, tomorrow, two hours from now? What's left to live for? There's a sign--thirteen miles to the next rest area! What does that tell you? Thirteen's unlucky. Is that an omen of some kind? Is that you, Elaina, calling me? Should I end it all? Are you still alive, in a better place? You're calling me, aren't you? Well...I'm coming. Ten minutes, Honey. Just give me ten minutes and I'll be with you.*

Before I knew it I was turning into that rest stop.

"Good," I said aloud after spotting a sign out front that read, "NO SECURITY GUARDS ON DUTY."

Slowly I idled around the block building to the farthest space in the back lot. The only other vehicles there were an eighteen-wheeler and an aging camping van; both parked a good distance behind me, near the restrooms. I nosed the RV close to a low fence that cordoned off a small pond and a scattering of thin pines, then I killed the engine. Like a deranged criminal about to embark on a wicked misdeed I shot quick looks side to side and out the rearview mirror. Then I leaned back into the seat and let my head fall against the headrest. I filled my lungs with air and let it out very slowly.

That's it. Here goes.

I stood up, leaned way over to the passenger side, removed the Glock from the glove compartment then sat back down. Looking down at the pistol, I massaged the handle.

Forty-one years had passed since I'd fired a gun. The last time had been in Nam while exchanging fire with *enemies* I didn't even know. Doing what I was told that night, fighting for my life and absolutely nothing else, three of the seven human beings I killed that year took their final breaths. I cannot tell you how horrible I felt, how indescribably hollow. But somehow, when it rose the next morning, the sun still shined a semblance of hope on my spirit. That hope was diluted of course, but as always, the new dawn still promised better things to come.

But this time--this day--was different. I looked up from the pistol in my hands to the new Florida sun before me. There was no hope in what I saw. Its light held no promise.

I raised the barrel and put it inside my mouth. The metal felt alien as I pointed it up, toward my brain. My heart battered the inside of my chest like it never had before. As I slowly increased the pressure on the trigger my tired eyes began to close. But then something happened. Just before my eyelids met, something stole my attention. Something flew out of one of the pine trees before me. My conscious mind unable to register what the odd shape was, I allowed my eyes to widen, just a tad. It was a bird. A large bird. It was flying straight toward the camper. My eyes rolled toward the top of the windshield as it flew closer. It was a pileated woodpecker, only the second one I'd ever seen. And just like the first one that morning with Elaina in Asheville, this one was making a racket.

It seemed to be scolding me from the time it left the tree until it disappeared over the roof of the camper. I was stunned.

Slowly, I withdrew the gun from my mouth. I set it on the console alongside me, and I said, "OK Elaina, I won't do it. Not yet."

Chapter 9

To say the two days after the Glock incident were trying, would be like calling a tsunami a ripple in the ocean. As I drove north toward the South Carolina coast, I also drove myself half mad. With the two sides of my brain pummeling each other with opposing thoughts, all I could try to do was keep steering the camper and hope the wrong side wouldn't win. Yes, with what I truly believed was Elaina's help, I had managed to fight back the suicide, but I was far from at ease. Part of my subconscious kept telling me I should have ended it all. Another part, the rational part, told me I'd done the right thing by not going through with my self-assassination.

But in all honesty, finding those good thoughts amongst all the negativity muddling up my mind, and then holding on to them for awhile, was not easy. There were times on both days that I was so close to panicking, I had to pull the hulking camper onto the highway's narrow shoulder. And that, my friend, is not only a tight fit but a very dangerous proposition as well.

The Winnebago was so close to the road that every passing car caused it to shimmy and every tractor-trailer made it shudder. But there was no choice. I was so mentally damaged, I literally could not see straight. When driving, I could not concentrate on anything in front, beside or behind me. After coming so close to killing myself in Florida, my own mind seemed alien and my body felt like it was someone else's. Each time I pulled off the road, I felt as if I was outside; floating high above and far away from the windshield, looking down into the camper, watching somebody that seemed only vaguely familiar. For obvious reasons I could not trust myself.

But I did survive those two days on the road. And with forty-eight hours and hundreds of miles between me and that Florida rest stop, my mind finally felt a little less fragile. On top of that, lady luck actually found the time to flash me a quick smile. She must have known how badly I needed to recreate myself, because when I reached my destination in South

Carolina, the campground I rolled into was the most serene I'd yet to come across. The place was just north of Myrtle Beach and all its hoopla, but you'd never have known it. It afforded as much privacy as I could possibly have hoped for. As soon as I came through the gate, I knew I wanted to spend the entire winter there.

One side of the grounds was nearly deserted, and each site had a buffer of dense trees and heavy underbrush. Making things better yet, I had no problem securing a spot on the farthest end. I could open my awning up, sit alongside the RV in the afternoons, and not a single passerby would be able to see me. Sure, it was warmer in Florida, but it is tolerable along "The Grand Stand." Many northerners on tight budgets happily spend the entire winter there. I know I was plenty happy to have found a place that felt both comfortable and reasonably secure.

Just before sunup most mornings, I'd lace up my jogging shoes and do three trips up and down the park's nature trail, which worked out to be just short of three miles. I rarely saw anybody back there at that time of day, and always considered it an added bonus when exchanging glances with the resident owl or a deer or two or three. Most days I tried to keep my mind occupied the best I could. I'd read, tinker with my lap-top, and nurse a few beers beneath the awning most afternoons.

Though I remained far from being a gadabout, I occasionally exchanged pleasantries with some of the other campers. Most of them were very nice retirees, older than me. Though I heartily believed none of them could possibly pose a threat, I forced myself to keep all conversations short. The only person I ever spoke to for more than a few minutes was an eighty-seven-year-old lady from Richmond, Virginia. Her name was Dixie Mae. She'd been employed at the same dry-cleaning store for the last twenty-seven years of her working life and had buried five husbands—the first when she was but seventeen. After a few weeks, she started calling me The New York Yankee, and I called her the black widow, which she thought was hilarious.

Dixie Mae had two small poodles named Beauregard and General, the latter of which was short for General Lee. Dixie could see I was lonely and kept suggesting that I should get a dog. At first I just blew off the idea, but as time went by, I kind of envied her for having two sidekicks to share her life with. I also thought it might be a good idea to have a little watchdog for when I headed west in the spring. At any rate, when I told her I might get one, Dixie Mae suggested I visit the animal shelter in Myrtle Beach. She told me where it was, and the next morning, after my run and requisite two cups of coffee, I unhooked the camper and headed down Highway 17.

Being I pretty much live in jeans, tee shirts, and sweaters I don't shop often, other than for groceries. When I do need to replenish my tees or sweaters, I drive myself crazy looking for a good deal and just the right fit. Knowing that, you can only imagine what it was like for me in that shelter. Adopting a dog would be no small commitment. The only thing I knew for sure was I wanted a small one. I was up and down the four long rows of cages I don't know how many times. Twice, I even snuck into a section where the dogs were not yet ready for adoption and the public wasn't allowed. I must have spent three hours poking around in that shelter. After a while the attendants started looking at me funny.

But there was one dog I kept coming back to--a two-year-old Jack Russell mix. She had the face of a tiny doe and the coloration of one also. But she had a questionable history. The paper notice on her cage warned:

My name is Penny.
I am not good with children, strangers, or other animals.
Though I haven't bitten anybody, I can be very aggressive and am best suited for a patient, mature owner.

Despite her obvious hang-ups, Penny looked healthy and was the perfect size for me and the camper. But what really attracted me, other than her beautiful tawny lashes, were her intelligent, chocolate eyes. Though they looked world-weary, I felt a connection every time I knelt in front of her. It was as if they said to me, "This just could possibly work, buddy boy, but don't think I'm going to do a complete turn-around for you or anyone else. I've got a few quirks; that's why I wound up here. Sorry, but don't expect me to change."

I decided to mull it over for a day or two. Penny (yeesh—I did not like that name) obviously had special needs, but I *did* like her. So on the way out of the shelter I stopped at the counter to ask a few questions. The three young girls at the desks seemed to be doing things far more important than acknowledging a prospective adopter. After waiting more than long enough I said, "Excuse me ladies, can one of you give me a little information."

One remained transfixed to something on her desk, and the other two looked at each other as if to say, "You help him." By this time I'm thinking, *Come on Eenie, Meenie, and Miney, let's get with the program! I don't see Moe around, so how about a little help here!*

Eventually the pale, freckled redhead grudgingly rose to her feet. As she slowly approached me she snapped her gum a few times and kept her dull eyes on a paper she was holding.

"Yes?" she said flatly, finally looking up at me.

"I was hoping you might tell me a little about one of the dogs."

"Which one would that be?"

"The Jack Russell mix, Penny. I want to think it over a day or two, but I was wondering if you could tell me a bit more about her issues."

Eenie, with her nose still to her desk, suddenly showed faint signs of life by saying ever so matter-of-factly, "Oh, the terrier with the attitude, she's scheduled to be euthanized tomorrow."

It turned out that Penny had been picked up by an animal control officer eighty-nine days prior. When he went to return it to the owners, they asked him if he'd take her to the shelter. They said they were moving to an apartment and wouldn't be allowed a dog. It seems the entire time they owned her she was tied outside their trailer next to a rancid little dog house. Sometimes her chain would become wrapped around a tree trunk, and for hours on end she'd nervously pace, back and forth around that tree. The officer also wrote in his report there was a well-worn path around it, and that surely there had been times during inclement weather when she'd not been able to reach her dog house. As a result Penny had become scared to death of thunder and lightning.

After hearing all this and more, my decision suddenly became a no-brainer. I knew right there and then I wanted to save this dog's life--and change her name. Immediately I took her outside for a short walk on the grass. When we came back into the office I not only paid the fee but also for a new leash, collar, and bag of dog food. At Eenie's suggestion, I also picked up a harness because Penny wasn't used to a leash. I'd already found that out on our walk when she'd pulled so hard a couple of times she choked herself.

On the way back to the campground Penny sat alongside me in the oversized passenger's seat. She studied me the whole way, seemingly assessing what she saw with her doggy logic.

When I backed the RV into my site Dixie Mae came over with General and Beauregard. Penny went absolutely Cujo— jumping up, barking, growling, and scratching on the window as if she wanted to tear the docile poodles apart. After explaining to Dixie Mae that the dog had problems, she thought it was big of me to have adopted her in spite of them. But after that episode, the only time Dixie and I talked anymore was on the rare occasions when one of us was without our pets.

I soon learned my new sidekick would bark, growl, or snarl at any living creature that ventured within a hundred yards of us. Size did not matter to her. She had an incurable case of the Napoleon Syndrome. Nevertheless, crazy as it sounds, a few weeks after she entered my life I renamed her, of all things, "Solace." Isn't that a first-degree misnomer, you might ask? Not really. Despite her aggression problems *solace* was exactly what she provided me with. She was, and still is, a very cerebral animal who despite her terrier stubbornness loves me deeply.

We connected from the get-go and she quickly became my second shadow. With all the time we were spending together I had less time to dwell on all my toxic fears and sorrows. To me she was a godsend, a four-legged gift all wrapped up in that tawny fur. That we had found each other had been nothing short of a blessing—to both of us. I had kept her alive and she was returning the favor, every day. Each morning I'd wake to wet, slobbering kisses all over my face. Who on earth could possibly start their days like that and at the same time entertain doomsday thoughts?

Unfortunately, as much as Solace helped, even she couldn't fend off all of my pain and distress. Even when they were on my mind's back burner, hurt and worry continued to blemish my spirit. I was no longer the person I used to be. And that will never change.

* * *

One night, after having Solace for about a month, I raised the courage to turn on my television set. This may not sound like a monumental achievement but to me it was. The last time I did it was before Elaina and I went to Stockholm. After we returned to that incomprehensible scene in our apartment, and our lives as we knew them were destroyed, we *needed* to distance ourselves from all that was going on. Besides watching a handful of educational shows, Jeopardy, or a movie now and then, the only reason we even owned a TV was to keep abreast of the news. Of course, like all other discerning individuals, when we always watched the news it was with eyes like hawks and our minds attuned to each and every word. We knew all too well that every sentence the corporate-owned talking heads delivered was tainted with the network's agenda. Everything they reported was slanted, propagandized, and full of sins of omission.

The TV was built into a small paneled wall above the front seats. And that first night I turned it on it was only a matter of minutes before I was reminded why I hadn't watched it for so long. The thing was barely warmed up when a newscaster said his network had been running a seven day critique of *Enough is Enough*. The messenger-boy/announcer said that this one was the final installment. He then went on to fill millions of viewer's heads with the network's take on Thomas Soles and his book.

"Tonight we are going to summarize Mister Soles' chapter about Wall Street. He says, and I quote, 'The single most destructive force to the faltering working-class is the greed-driven stock market and its major investors. Think how much better off the huge majority of Americans would be if all corporations were owned by all the people rather than just those with the most disposable income. The trillions of dollars that are bilked from the over-worked, under-paid populous every year would go into their own pockets rather than those of the chosen few who control two-thirds of this country's wealth. No longer would it be necessary to artificially inflate the cost of goods and services every year for the sake of dividends. Not only would the price of everything, from fingernail clippers to housing, not rise, they would tumble to levels you would not dream possible.

How much do you think it costs footwear companies, for example, to put together a pair of gym shoes assembled in some third-world country for third-world wages? The very same sneakers that sit on the shelves of another company's store until you buy them for sixty, eighty, a hundred dollars or more. The cost of production probably isn't more than six or seven dollars--if that. Why is it that the information concerning such corporate costs are more closely guarded than the U.S. Government's top secrets?'

Up to that point in the broadcast, the news anchor had been strictly business. He'd read the excerpt in as professional a voice as he could muster. But then he changed his tune as well as his tone. It had become time to slant. He first took off his glasses and slowly lowered them to his desk. Then he looked straight into the eye of the camera and America, and massaged his temples as if exhausted and blown away by what he'd just read. Finally, in a far gentler, down-homey voice that was meant to endear his audience, he said, "Friends, it is the belief of this station that words such as these are nothing short of national threats. They are treasonous. In this blasphemous book I am holding in my hands, Thomas Soles has singlehandedly attempted to discredit our tried and proven capitalistic system. He is trying to diminish *our* system--*our* method of doing things

70

that has built this great country into what it is today. No wonder this book is being yanked off store shelves everywhere. No wonder Mister Soles is on the run, hiding out. I'd be hiding if..."

By that time I'd had it. I shut off the television, lowered Solace from my lap to the floor, and went to the kitchen area to make popcorn. As the kernels popped and the brown bag expanded in the microwave, all I could do was pivot my head side to side ever so slowly.

Here's a multi-million-dollar puppet in a two-thousand dollar suit telling the rest of the country how good they have it-- at a time when so many of them have been priced out of their last dream. What may be even scarier yet is that hoards of those very same people are buying what that carpetbagger's selling. Yup...I'm sure he's succeeding. His sponsors and all the rest will love him. I'm sure there are a few million more people who now consider me a modern-day Benedict Arnold. My god, how do they keep petting the same dog that keeps biting them?

Chapter 10

The next day two unfortunate events took place at The Carolina Oaks Campground. Number one, Dixie Mae said goodbye to me. For the first time in over twenty winters she had to go back to Virginia early. Though it had grown increasingly difficult over the past ten years, this time she couldn't afford to stay until April first. I thought about giving her the site fee, but I knew this proud, old survivor would never have taken it. For all the years she'd been coming she had only stayed in our treed section of the campground because it was cheaper than the others. That's why she and I were the only ones on our side of the huge circular dirt road. Everybody wanted to stay where it's sunny. You see, where we were the sky was always green, with leaves. We received virtually no sunlight. And as cool, and sometimes downright cold, as South Carolina gets in winter, nobody wanted to be in those trees. Well, almost nobody.

Standing in the road, waving goodbye as she pulled away that morning, I was not a happy camper. But bad as I felt losing my only human contact, things were about to get worse. In a mere few hours my spirits would plummet to even lower depths.

It was early afternoon. I was inside the camper reading an email from my editor, Denise Solchow. She said, despite being dropped by the two mega-booksellers, sales of *Enough is Enough* still had been "robust." I was no longer following the rankings, but Denise said it was still ninth on the New York Times Best Seller List. It had been number one for fifty-something weeks but had fallen because of the boycott. She asked me what to do with the most recent royalty check, and I'd just finished telling her to hold on to it when Solace started raising all kinds of hell.

She was up front on the passenger seat woofing, growling, carrying on like she always did when she smelled, saw, or heard something. I quickly finished my response to Denise then got up and peeked out the windshield. Just as I did, the biggest motor home I'd ever seen stopped dead in the road, right smack in front of my Winnebago.

"Shhh, shhh, OK!" I said to Solace, pulling her back, trying to keep her from clawing ruts into the dashboard. I put her on the carpeted floor, but that did nothing to stave off her fitful barking.

The luxury RV before me was the size of a Greyhound tour bus. It was just like the ones the big-name bands and all their groupies trip across the country in, and just as elegant. This was the type of diesel motor home that sells for half a million dollars.

Looking directly into a side window, maybe twenty feet in front of me, I could see what must have been the dining area. A huge crystal chandelier swayed heavily and beyond that, I saw ornate gilded mirrors on what appeared to be mahogany wall cabinets. The custom black paint-job on the outside, with all its gold swooshes and slashes, shone brighter than a cadet's shoes on graduation day. This so-called "camper," with Michigan plates, was more like a presidential suite on wheels.

Oh shit! I'll bet he's going to back right in there. What the hell's he doing on this side of the park? Ohhh, I know...I'll bet the sunny side's all filled up.

Sure enough, he did back in--directly across the road. But first he unhooked the glistening new Hummer he'd been towing. All decked out in designer shorts; a golf shirt with some kind of logo over his heart; sockless loafers; and a cell phone holster at the ready, the chubby little man shouted orders to his equally chubby little wife. He had the poor woman jumping back and forth all over that campsite. I had to feel bad for her. She would be right in the middle of doing what she'd been told, and the red-faced dictator would start shouting out new orders, which she'd promptly respond to. After ten minutes of watching all this I got a little tired of it. Solace was still raising hell so I put her in the bedroom and closed the door. I grabbed a smoke, popped open a beer, and sat outside under the awning.

"Whew," I said to myself, "at least they can't see me out here, with all these bushes." But I was not happy.

A short time later, after all the commotion ended, I figured I'd get another beer and bring Solace outside. My nerves being what they were, I was startled when I rose out of the lawn chair.

"Hey, what do you say big boy?"

It was the take-charge guy. He had come from behind the bushes and caught me off guard. He had a resonant deep voice that mismatched his stature, and I actually flinched.

"Whoooa! Relax man, didn't mean to scare you. Thought I'd just come over and introduce myself."

"Oh, that's OK. I'm fine. Just didn't hear you coming is all. I'm ah, Frank...Frank Reynolds."

I really did not want to shake this man's hand, but he did go out of his way to come over and introduce himself. Reluctantly, I extended my hand and was immediately sorry I had. There was an uncomfortable hesitation before he accepted it. The delay had been deliberate, and I damn well knew it.

When we finally did shake he studied my face far more than another man normally would have. "I'm J. Henry Logsdon," he said, "of Grosse Pointe, Michigan, and Vail, Colorado."

He then let go of my hand. And I was glad, not only because I didn't like him but because his was all clammy and soft as a fashion-model's. He immediately pointed to the front of my RV and said, "I see you're from Newwww Yorrrk."

He said New York as if it had put a rotten taste in his mouth, as if rolling the R awhile would dispel all its unpleasantness.

"Well...yes, I'm from Queens--Flushing to be exact." *Oh shit*, I thought, *I didn't mean to tell him that.*

"That's a damn good place to be *from* isn't it?"

"Excuse me?"

"Well, you know, Newwww Yorrrk isn't exactly the garden spot of the world, if you know what I mean."

"Where do you get off talking like...you know what, forget all that, who do you think you are coming over here and..."

He interrupted me with a new smirk on his face--this one bigger than the two he'd been wearing both times he said New York. "Who do I think I am? I'll tell you exactly who *I* am, *my friend*, J. Henry Logsdon."

This was a man who'd obviously been protected by his wealth and social status all his life. Nobody who lived in the real world would ever dream of giving a stranger such shit-- particularly a stranger a head taller and three times as fit. I tried to fight back the creed of the city streets I grew up in—talk the talk, walk the walk. I wanted to give this prima donna a good pounding. My fists balled themselves at my sides, but I held them back. I was just about to really tell him off but he spoke first, and what he said knocked me for a loop.

"Frank Reynolds, huh? I don't think so. I know who you are, buster. Why the hell do you think I bothered coming over here? I saw the plates on this heap. You're the only one on this entire side of the park. I figured it just might be you, hiding out. Shit, the whole country knows you're running scared in an RV. You've been all over the news. Last time I saw your picture was just last night. You can run, traitor, but you can't hide."

The shroud of fear I'd struggled with for so many weeks tightened around me like an iron straightjacket. I didn't even notice the driving rain that had begun drumming on the awning, or the sudden drop in temperature. I barely heard Solace going berserk inside the camper. Moving closer now, I went eye to beady eye with him. Speaking slowly, measuring the distance between each word I said, "I want you the fuck out of here little man, right fucking now!"

He didn't budge. He didn't flinch. He stayed right where he was. His face flushed crimson with hate, and he started shouting, "Do you have any idea how much money I've lost this year because of you and that so-called *book* of yours? Do you have a clue how much that propaganda piece of shit has hurt the market? Do you know how much *YOU* took from me?"

He then paused, shaking his breakfast-sausage finger at me. His entire body began to tremor from all the hate and anger built up inside. Then he erupted. Saliva spraying everywhere he hollered, "Almost two million is how much! Two fucking million dollars, *Soles*!"

Like an immigrant reverting to his native language when blistering anger overcomes him, my New York accent suddenly resurrected from the days of my youth. Nobel Prize or no Nobel Prize, I no longer gave a shit about rolling my R's or any of the rest of it.

"That's it, you son-of-a-bitch, get yaw ass outta heah, NOW! I'll break you in half you selfish little piss-ant! Move it! Get goin'!"

He started backpedaling, fast, and I helped him gain momentum with two palms to the chest.

Solace was yipping and yelping, scratching desperately at the bedroom window as if she was fighting for her balance on a sheet of ice. Logsdon's wife was outside their motor home now; screaming for him to get inside. "Go on, you low-life bahstad. Keep movin'. That's it, tell yaw story walkin'."

Stopping on the other side of the road, standing in the downpour, he shook his fist and hollered, "There are millions of us, Soles! We're going to get you, you son of a bitch! You don't believe it...turn your computer on. Check out soleswatch.com, you'll see."

Wiping the rain from his face, his last words before retreating were, "You haven't heard the last of me, you loser! I promise! Remember my name...J. Henry Logsdon!"

With his name still echoing through the sprawl of rain-drenched trees, I dropped the single-finger salute I'd been pumping madly. I turned around, picked up my cigarettes and empty beer can then climbed back into the camper.

I let Solace out of the bedroom. She sped right back to the passenger seat, still carrying on. I fell into the sofa and turned on my laptop. With shaky hands I lit a smoke, took a long draw, and then laid it in the ashtray.

Sure as hell, soleswatch.com came up. In bold black letters across the top of the first page it read, "PUBLIC ENEMY NUMBER 1." Just beneath that was a row of five sketches-- every one of my face. Graphic looking depictions of how I might look with a mustache, a beard, or both. They had me with long hair, short hair, and even a shaved head. The text beneath the pictures ranted about how I was single-handedly costing the U.S. economy billions of dollars. Of course, there was no mention about how their stock market had just finished a banner year when the rest of America had been wallowing in another recession. There was no mention of the hundreds of billions of taxpayer dollars that shored up Wall Street's stellar returns, while virtually nothing trickled down to those who had footed the bill.

Fuck it, I thought, *I can't read any more of this crap! Where's their blogs section?*

But before clicking on that, I saw something called Soles-sightings. I clicked on it, and what I saw made me feel like the camper's walls had instantly shrunk and were closing in around me.

Just that quickly, I felt trapped, as if I was constrained in a small box. I was mortified. My palms became sweaty, and I suddenly wasn't getting enough oxygen. My heart stuttered; then missed a beat. When it kicked back in, it felt as if it might shatter its ribbed cage.

I jumped to my feet in a panic and rushed for the door. I had to get outside-- fast. I needed fresh air. I tried to breath but couldn't. It was as if I'd swallowed something too large or too sticky, and it had blocked my airway. I was becoming light-headed.

When I got outside I just stood there, hands on my hips. For I don't know how long, I sucked, gasped, and labored to get my breath back. Finally, I did. The respirations were shallow at first, but they soon became full-blown breaths. I stayed outside for a while longer after that and tried to compose myself. When I eventually did, I went back inside to the computer.

Again, I saw on the screen the map of the United States. Again I saw a route traced from the Northeast south--the exact same route Elaina and I had taken since we'd left home two months earlier. A footnote beneath the map said the path of my "retreat" was based on information provided by anonymous individuals who had sighted my camper. Just above the footnote was a small picture of the Winnebago—sitting in the Jersey dealer's lot before we'd bought it. Next to that was another picture--a photograph of my New York license plate.

At the very bottom of the page was an obscure, fine-print disclaimer. Only two lines long it read, "This web site is in no way meant to encourage anyone to bring harm to Thomas Soles. He has not broken any laws that we are aware of, and to the best of our knowledge, is not a fugitive from justice."

Less than twenty minutes later the awning was rolled up, Solace had done her business outside, everything inside was secured, and we rolled out of The Carolina Oaks Campground. That was now the second time I'd rushed out of a campground. Again, I didn't even stop to ask for a refund of my site fee.

Chapter 11

As Solace and I motored down U.S. 17 in the gray rain at dusk, I tried to shove J. Henry Logsdon away again--this time from my mind. When he and all my hate and anger began to fade, I vowed to somehow keep my head together. I could not allow myself to fall to pieces again. I could not suspect that every car behind me and all those coming at me were would-be assassins on the hunt. But that wouldn't be easy. Knowing what I did now, about that website, added a lot more black paint to my dark, dangerous predicament.

While trying to fight back all the unfriendly scenarios lined up outside my mind, I made my way through North Myrtle's business district. Miles of light, from miles of free-standing businesses and strip-malls, splayed a spectrum of colors on all the puddles and wet concrete. My wipers, now set on low, easily kept up with the surrendering rain. Exhausted as she was from all the chaos at the campground, Solace slept soundly beside me. An RV in front of me stopped for a red light, and I followed suit. As my headlights illuminated his Florida license plate, the orange and all, I suddenly got an idea. I thought of something that just might make my Winnebago a tad more anonymous.

Why not take off the front plate? Why let anyone approaching me see I'm from New York? A lot of states only require one in the back, Florida's not the only one. What are the odds a cop is going to notice? This thing is thirty feet long! If a cruiser comes toward me, what're the odds whoever's inside is going to turn his head after passing—notice a New York plate, and say, "Hmmm...where's his other plate. He didn't have one on the front, did he?" I don't think so! That's never going to happen. Not only that, but wherever I get a site, I always back in. If a park only offers drive-thru sites, I don't stay there, simple as that. When I do find the right place, anybody walking by the front bumper won't have a clue where I'm from. The benefits hugely outweigh the risks. Done deal! I'll stop at the next gas station; as long as it's not one of those two companies I boycott. I'll fill up the tank, then pull in back and take off the plate.

That's exactly what I did. When I finished, I put the plate and screwdriver away, swung onto State Road 501, and headed toward Florence in the darkness. Much of 501 is desolate and very eerie at night, and I was damn glad to be on it. I decided that well before picking up I-95 South again, I'd drive only under the cover of darkness for a few days.

That night my new travelling partner and I ate up more than six-hundred miles of road before giving it up near DeFuniak Springs, Florida. Yes, believe it or not, Florida! Time and again, while driving those wee hours beneath the southern stars, I looked at Solace sleeping beside me. I can't tell you how comforting it was to have her company. No longer did I feel so alone. I now had a compatriot who, despite her size, would willingly fight to her death alongside me. I also had something else to *live* for, which I badly needed. Think about it. What were the chances of ever finding a semblance of normalcy in my future? Any hopes I had left of improving my sense of well-being were all but gone. They seemed to be dwindling with every passing day, hour, and minute. I *needed* another reason to live.

A few times, when I glanced over at Solace that night, I felt another emotion. Right alongside comfort, *envy* kept shouldering its way into my psyche. Not jealousy of course, just plain old envy. Each of those times I couldn't help feeling like Frank Baum's cowardly lion in The Wizard of Oz. When I looked at Solace those times I couldn't help but to wish I had half her courage.

* * *

The reason I doubled back to Florida was because it was warm and there were two full months of winter left. I'd thought about Arizona, but didn't think the desert would be for me. I entertained thoughts of Brownsville, Texas, on the Mexican border, but realized I needed to hole up somewhere away from the beaten path. Knowing that the Florida Panhandle is a heck of a lot more like Georgia than it is South Florida, I hoped to find a small out-of-the-way town.

It was still dark out, around five AM, when I rolled into a convenience store/gas station fifteen-miles east of DeFuniak Springs. Not only was the needle on my fuel gauge flirting with the "empty" mark, but the windshield was enshrouded with DOA insects. There were so many bugs that when I hit the windshield washer and turned on the wipers, the result was a solid smear across the glass. We'd been on the road twelve hours, and I was beyond tired.

A forest of pines--black as the pre-dawn sky--surrounded "Jasper's iffy Stop" (the J was missing); and on the other side of the deserted two-lane, was more of the same. This was logging country and not much more. It was no surprise that the pump area and parking lot were also deserted.

I climbed out of the camper on uncertain legs, inserted the gas nozzle, and walked Solace beyond the glow of the station's lights. On a spit of grass alongside the dark pine forest, I waited for Solace to do her things. Listening to the incessant chirp of a nearby cricket congregation, I tried to focus my blurred vision on the stars overhead. A nearby turkey gobbled in the woods, a real treat for an old city boy to hear. But then I saw something. And it was far from a treat.

A mud splattered pickup truck with four huge wheels pulled up to the storefront. The tailgate was open and there was a flat-bottomed aluminum boat sticking way out the back. After killing the headlights, a tall, hulking figure slowly got out. He stood there a few seconds staring at my RV. He then adjusted his ball cap, hitched up his jeans, looked side to side once, and sauntered over to the Winnebago. Scratching his behind a couple of times, he slowly walked alongside it; inspecting it closely.

Then, as if it was nobody's business but his own, he removed the nozzle from my camper and hung it back on the pump.

I was going to yell, but I'd learned many years earlier, in Southeast Asia, just how valuable the element of surprise can be. I figured now, if I could sneak back into the driver's door, I could get a hold of my pistol before he even knew I was there.

The guy then stopped in the back, surely seeing the license plate. Next, he went around to the far side where I could no longer see him. After giving Solace's leash a slight tug, we did a quick half-trot back over there.

Damn, I thought, as we made our way toward the pump island, *what the hell was I thinking. Middle of nowhere, pitch-black out here, not a soul around other than the store clerk, and I'm out here without the Glock. Shit! What an idiot I am!*

Then Solace blew my plan wide open. From her low vantage point she'd seen the guy's legs moving on the far side of the camper. She did what she did best and went ballistic. Before we were close enough to the door, the big man had come around to the front! Right on the other side of the concrete island when we reached it, face to face with us, he said, "Whoooah, take it easy killer!"

Then, smearing a grin across a face wide as those atop Rushmore, he said, "Now, just you take it easy big boy."

He then turned his head to the side and spit tobacco juice through his teeth. It splashed on the cement about eight feet away. As he did this, my eyes were drawn to a holster at his side. Yes, he was packing. The flap on the holster was unbuttoned, which wasn't a good sign. On top of that, this guy was huge. He had to be about six-eight, crowding three hundred pounds. He was carrying a little extra weight around his midsection, but he was one powerful looking man. His green cap said "Remington" across the front, and it was tilted back on his head. A shock of thick brown hair hung from beneath it, covering his forehead. His blue jeans were rolled up, and where they met his knees they were wet. Standing there in his bare feet this guy looked like a cross between Paul Bunyon and Huckleberry Finn. I didn't know what to make of him, and what he did after spitting did nothing to calm my nerves.

He turned back towards us then drew up his right hand. In the process he brushed up against the holster flap. For sure I thought he was reaching for his pistol. I was just about to jump on him, try to bury my thumbs into his eyes. I'd once seen a very small friend of mine do exactly that in a bar fight and totally disable a man twice his size. But thank god I didn't have to resort to such a measure. After brushing the flap he finished his motion and simply wiped the residue saliva from his mouth.

"Ya'll ain't from around here, I see."

"No...we're not. We're just passing through; just making a pit stop."

Solace was now on top of the cement island, still carrying on like she wanted to tear him apart. As I held her back with the leash, he crouched in front of her and gently offered his hand.

"Be careful." I said, "She may very well try to bite you."

"Naw, she won't bite me, will you girl?" he said, ever so slowly easing his down-turned hand toward her.

I could not believe what I was seeing and hearing. This fortyish giant was like one of those animal whisperers. A moment later Solace actually stopped all her barking and sniffed his hand. Soon he was stroking her head, and I felt a whole lot better.

Still down on his haunches, looking up at me now, he said, "Hope you don't mind, I pulled that there nozzle out of your gas tank. You were up to a hundred and two bucks and fuel was spillin' all over the concrete there."

"No, no, heck no! Thank you very much. I'd thought for sure it had had an automatic shut-off."

"I've been tellin' ole Jasper in there," he said, nodding at the store, "he needs to update. But hell, nobody round here's got that kinda money, 'specially Jasper. Only thing he's got for sure is a missing letter on his sign and a gambling problem."

Rising to his feet he put out his hand. "Name's Franklin Dewitt. I live just down the road. Where you headin'? I see you got New York plates."

I shook his hand and immediately knew how that J. Henry Logsdon character must have felt when I was fool enough to shake his. I felt like a Boy Scout shaking with his scout leader.

"I'm Jay, Jay Henry," was the best I could come up with at the moment. "Solace and I are just bouncing around a bit. In the spring I want to go out West, but for the time being, we just want to stay somewhere warm. The main thing, right now, is to find a nice quiet campground. We've been driving all night, and I've had it."

"Well, Fallin' Waters State Park is back just a ways, off I-10. They have camp sites there. There's a little bitty mom and pop place just the other side of DeFuniak Springs, too, but none of 'em would be open for at least a couple of hours. Can't be any later than five, five-thirty about now."

Checking my watch I said, "Yup, you're right, it's only five-twenty. But that's OK. I'll just pay for the gas. We'll figure something out. Thanks for shutting off the pump and..."

"Whooa, hold on," Franklin interrupted. "Like I said, my place ain't far, just a couple a miles from here. You want to, you and Solace here can set up there for the day, get caught up on sleep, whatever."

Under normal circumstances I'd never consider such an offer, especially from such an imposing stranger. Granted, the guy seemed to be on the up and up, but you never know. On the other hand, was I better off parking somewhere—here in the middle of nowhere--for two hours until the state park or the other place opened up? Who was to say a bored country sheriff might not happen along with an arsenal of questions? I didn't even know if it was legal to have a loaded gun in my glove compartment.

"Look," he said as I deliberated, "it's up to you, but I got sixty acres in the woods. It's just me there, ain't no wife around or nothin'. Got a pond out back that's full of bream and bass, and the place is a lot prettier than those campgrounds. A lot more private, too."

Bingo! The word "private" lit up inside my head like neon. It might just be the perfect place to get a good day's sleep. What did I have to lose? Even though I only knew this man for five, maybe ten minutes, I somehow couldn't help but to trust him. Of course, I'd still lock all the doors before going to sleep. And if by some chance my instincts proved wrong, I still had the Glock.

"I really appreciate the offer, and I don't mean to be a pain in the ass, but if you have any loose dogs or anything, Solace would never let me sleep."

"Don't worry. I ain't got no dogs. Just buried my Missy 'bout two months ago. It'll be a long spell before I get another dog. Can't take that kinda hurt, if you know what I mean."

That was it! The way I saw it, anybody with the capacity to truly love a dog like he seemed to, couldn't be all that bad. The fact that Solace actually warmed up to him also threw a lot of weight into my decision. I offered to pay Franklin Dewitt but did not press the issue when he refused to accept money. His overgrown boyish face actually looked disappointed, maybe even a tad insulted. In my neck of the woods, a monetary gesture would be expected; in his, it obviously would not be tolerated.

I still had to pay for the gas, and Franklin wanted to buy some chewing tobacco, so the three of us headed toward the store. As we approached his truck, with the boat in back, I asked him if he'd been out doing some night fishing.

"Nuh uh," he said, "take a look in the boat." And I did. There was a hand-held spotlight wired to an automobile battery in there, along with about a twelve-foot pole. Stretched out next to the pole, and just about as long, were two freshly-killed Florida alligators. Just like Franklin's knees, their bodies were still soaking wet. The storefront lights eerily reflecting off the hulking primeval creatures. With both of them lying on their bellies, the light seemed to glisten off their wide, treaded backs in a thousand different directions.

It turned out Franklin Dewitt was a true gentleman--a genuine prince. For far too long, I'd believed that the bigger the man, the bigger his ego and attitude had to be. Boy, did Franklin disprove that nonsense. Solace and I went on to spend most of the winter at his place, and he could not have been more accommodating. The only money he would accept was thirty dollars a month for the electric I used.

When he wasn't using his boat, he'd leave it alongside the six-acre pond for me and Solace. And it was no accident that, whenever we felt like using it, there was always fresh bait, a tackle box, and a well-cared-for fishing rod sitting in it. Whenever he roasted a wild hog or barbequed meat, he'd always cook a few bass or bream fillets and bring them to me. If I happened to be outside the camper when he was heading to Jasper's iffy Stop, he'd always ask if I needed cigarettes, beer, or anything else.

Franklin's place was two miles off the paved county road. The only way in was a dirt road through the thick pines and palmettos. If it was possible anywhere, this was the perfect place to try to simmer my fears and pain a bit. A place I never left except for the occasional trip to Jasper's or to dump the camper's sewage. It was a refuge, so to speak, a place where I could disassociate myself from the rest of the world.

I never once looked at a newspaper and did not miss them. Not reading all those slanted views allowed me a refreshing hiatus from my usual early-morning funks. My only connection to the so-called real world was the cell phone. There was no DSL for the laptop, no cable for the TV. Franklin didn't even own a television, and that certainly added to my sense of security. He said he once put up an antenna, but it was worthless.

The only other structure back there was the remnants of an old, wood-framed cracker house. Totally collapsed by now, his great-grandfather had built the place in 1901, when he was seventeen-years old. Boar and deer were still in good supply, and on the occasions Franklin killed one, I totally understood. He was a man who lived off his land and earned very little money when he was off it. That's why he poached alligators, had a nuisance trapper's license to remove them, and totally disregarded all hunting season dates. As for me, I stuck to my jogging routine on his dirt road, and wrote the entire first half of this book during my stay.

In early March, on the last night before Solace and I were to move on, I learned something else about Franklin Levi Dewitt— something else he occasionally did for money. Something, had I known the night I met him, dog-tired or not, I would have sped out of Walton County so fast the camper would have gone airborne.

He and I were lounging in Adirondack chairs on the deck behind his cabin. The huge Florida sun had dropped beyond the tree line, leaving a pale pink smear on the fading sky above it.

Franklin and I, nursing cold ones, watched a great blue heron wrestle a small flapping fish he'd just plucked from the pond. Franklin dropped his massive arm over the side of his chair and gently massaged Solace's ear, as she lay sprawled between us on the cypress planking. The crickets had begun their usual chorus and Franklin said, "You know, Jay, I'm a lot like that there heron."

Hating the fact that after all he'd done for me, and all the time I'd spent at his place, I still couldn't tell him my real name, I said, "What do you mean?"

"Well, just like that bird, there are times I have to travel around to hunt down my next meal."

"Hunt down?"

"Yeah, in a way, I'm just like that bird. I've been gone the last four days haven't I?"

"Yeahhh?"

"I sure as hell didn't want to go nowhere. But sometimes, when the money's low and the opportunity comes a knockin', I gotta go for it."

"What did you do, remove a few gators for somebody?"

He tipped his Remington cap farther back, scratched his forehead then said, "Naw, I've been out to Pensacola. Did a job for somebody I know. A little tracking, like that heron did to run down that shiner. Only I hunted down a man."

Jesus Christ, I'm thinking now, *no, no, don't let this be true. It can't be! No way could I have been wrong about this guy all along. I refuse to believe he's involved in some kind of clandestine shit? Wait, could I have been wrong? Could he be some kind of murder-for-hire head-case? Is that why he stays out here, all alone in the woods? Damn, the last night we're here and this has to happen.*

"Look, Franklin, I said, unable to hide my concern, "I don't know what you're involved in, but maybe it's best I don't. I don't want to…"

He then interrupted me with a howling laugh. "Hell's fire, Jay, what do you think I am, some kinda mass murderer?"

He let go of Solace's ear and gave me a little jab on the shoulder. "I just do a little work for an ex-sheriff I know. His name's George Tyson. When he retired he opened up a little business in Pensacola. From time to time, I just help him out a little is all. Hot damn, you're a pisser!"

Lucky for me it was getting dark. The hot blood rushing to my face surely turned it scarlet. I felt like an A-1, top-of-the-line, gold-plated idiot. And a traitor as well.

How, I asked myself, *could I ever have thought he might be capable of such malevolence?*

You can only imagine how relieved I was. Think about it, one minute you believe you may be sitting alone, in the woods, with a possible axe murderer; the next you find out your imagined death-sentence was just a ridiculous misunderstanding. It's like going from doomsday to Christmas day in a flash.

Unfortunately, the huge flood of relief I'd felt dried up as quickly as it had arrived. What Franklin told me next made all my previous imaginings seem like petty, inconsequential concerns.

Still wearing an embarrassed smile, I said, "Alright, alright, Franklin! I'm sorry. I guess my mind was off in the twilight zone for a minute there." Then, hoping to quickly switch subjects, I said, "How do you help your buddy out? What do you do for him?"

"Between me, you, and the wall, Jay, I sometimes do a little bounty hunting. That's what I was doing for ole George the past few days."

Oh my good God! A bounty hunter! Shhhit! He still called me Jay, but is he just toying with me? Maybe his buddy found out about Soleswatch.com. Maybe Franklin himself threw me under the bus. Maybe in Pensacola they were contacting bloggers on that fucking site; making deals. Maybe Franklin IS a hit-man after all! He might've been up there with that guy lining up as many prospective customers as possible. If they could get a half--dozen clients to pay for a single job, why not-- that's what they call good business nowadays. Oh hell, what am I going to do? I don't know what to think anymore. Am I totally losing it? It is possible I'm not his sacrificial lamb. Is it possible that, even if my hunch is right, Franklin would never do me in? Is my hunch just that-a hunch-a sick perverse hunch?

Having no idea what was going to happen next, I wanted to run off that deck so fast that Solace would have had a hard time keeping up with me. But I couldn't. With as nonchalant an air as I could muster, I slid a cigarette from my pack, lit it, and mixed smoke with my words while saying, "Well, Franklin, whatever a guy's got to do to bring home the bacon. Things sure as hell aren't easy anymore."

I stayed with him another twenty minutes or so. Male etiquette being what it is, if I had rushed off without finishing my beer he'd have known something was up. I kept the conversation flowing with small talk, hoping to somewhat smooth out the uncomfortable situation I'd created. Nevertheless, I remained as alert as an eight-point buck during hunting season.

Franklin did not whip out a chainsaw, an axe, or any weapon meant for my destruction, but I still had one more night in the camper. Sure, I could have taken off right then, just turned over the engine and hit the road. But two things held me back. Number one, if Franklin had wanted to finish me off, odds were he would have done it right there on the deck--behind his house. There would have been no better place to execute the misdeed. Secondly, after all he'd done for me and Solace, as close as I'd connected with him; I seriously doubted he would do that for money. Not the fine human being I had come to know. Nevertheless, when I put the lights out in the camper that night, after kissing Elaina's cap, I laid the loaded Glock beside it.

I couldn't fall asleep for two hours. Oh, I knew Solace would have alerted me had Franklin approached the camper, but there was yet another thing eating at me. With all that was running through my mind when I said goodbye to him, I felt like it was a hollow goodbye. I wanted to make it seem as heartfelt as it would have been had I not known he was a bounty hunter. But I knew it didn't come across that way. Franklin hadn't acted as if he was disappointed, but I know my sincerity had to seem somewhat fraudulent. He surely must have picked up on that.

Though I'd fallen asleep later than usual, I still awoke at my usual time. The old cerebral alarm clock rang at 5:02. My first decision of the day was to forgo my morning jog--*just* to be on the safe side. After a quick shower, and all the rest, I fired up the engine. It was still black as pitch back there. All the lights in Franklin's cabin were still out. Slowly, being as quiet as possible, I followed my low beams across the damp grass to where the dirt road began. As I pulled onto it, I said to Solace in the co-pilot's seat, "What the heck do you suppose that is, partner?"

Standing dead center in the narrow road was an upside down, white, five-gallon plastic bucket. Taped to it was a paper envelope.

I put the camper in park, looked in all four directions then hurriedly opened the door.

"Stay." I told Solace. Then I climbed out.

Before stepping into the camper's beams, I looked around a second time. Then I scurried to the bucket. After picking it up, I quick-stepped out of the lights—back to the side of the road. There, in the darkness, I pulled off the soggy, duct-taped envelope. I then put the bucket down alongside the road and pulled myself back into the camper.

After turning on the overhead light, I found a note inside the envelope. The words, scrawled with a ballpoint pen, were a bit runny from the moisture, but they were legible. The note said, "Keep in touch my friend. And take care of that puppy. I wrote my cell number on the bottom of this note. If you ever need something don't wait ta call me. I'll be pulling for you, Tom."

I gently laid the paper note on the console, and a small smile pulled at my lips. I rotated my head once or twice. A moment later, as I slowly followed the headlights down Franklin Dewitt's long, dark driveway, my vision became blurry. It had nothing to do with the sleep in my eyes.

Chapter 12

After I left Franklin's place, that early morning daylight took its sweet time coming. When it finally did arrive, it revealed a low, dark, tragic-looking sky. Solace and I were coming up on Pensacola when dawn finally arrived, along with a driving rain. Leave it to me to pick such a dreary day to return to a life of worry.

Solace and I managed to cover four-hundred miles that day, but it was slow going on Interstate 10. Up to this point, I'd found Sundays the best day of the week to travel, but that rain really slowed us down. Heading west, we lost the most time sloshing through Mobile, Biloxi--with all its casinos, New Orleans, and Baton Rouge. What would normally have taken eight hours took ten.

Needless to say, after all the peaceful time I'd spent at Franklin's sanctuary, I didn't exactly relish feeling like a moving target again. For the first time since Elaina and I took to the road, I found myself seriously entertaining thoughts of settling down somewhere. Being it was now early March, winter would soon use up the last of its cold fury. I could turn around; head northeast; follow the Appalachians all the way up to Maine. I could buy the small, isolated place Elaina and I had dreamed about so many times. I could go way up into those North Woods, where there was nary a soul. Yes, that's what I would do. Just before stopping outside Lake Charles, Louisiana that late afternoon, I decided I definitely *would* settle in Maine-- but not yet. It was a tad too early. Though my life surely would have been less precarious had Solace and I headed straight up there, I really wanted to see Colorado, Wyoming, and Montana. They were three of the four states I'd always most wanted to visit. Alaska was the other one, but things being what they were, that would have been too much of a stretch.

I knew that forging ahead to those Rocky Mountain States wouldn't improve my sense of security like going to Maine would have, but it was now or never. We could make it in three days, four without pushing. I decided to go for it.

Late that afternoon I stopped at a campground office just east of Lake Charles. After paying the fee, I drove beneath a canopy of dismal dripping oaks to our assigned site. As I looked around while plowing through a succession of muddy puddles, I wasn't the least bit disappointed that the place was deserted. For the first time that day I felt at ease. And minutes later, after backing into my spot and taking Solace out to do her business, I felt even better.

For the first time in over two months, I typed Soleswatch.com into my laptop. It still had PUBLIC ENEMY NUMBER 1 across the top of the page and the five sketches beneath it, but when I pulled up the tracking map I let out an audible sigh of relief. That too hadn't changed. The last place I'd been spotted was still Myrtle Beach. With that news, and the campground empty as it was, I slept almost as well as most nights at Franklin Dewitt's.

At seven the following morning, after feeding Solace and downing a bowl of raisin bran, we rolled out of the campground. The weather was as bad as the day before, and the farther we drove the more it deteriorated. Nevertheless, with the windshield wipers working overtime, we pressed on.

At eleven AM we hit Houston. We also hit some of the worst traffic I'd ever encountered anywhere. The highway formed a wide loop around that city, and I had to get on the thing to pick up I-45 North. I can't tell you how many lanes were in, above, or below that loop, but if you ever want a totally overwhelming, absolutely dizzying driving experience, be sure to put this one at the top of your list.

What made matters even worse was not only the weather, but the fact I was driving a thirty-foot home on wheels. Driving one of those clumsy things in foul weather, particularly on windy days, is no easy task. It can be one heck of a nerve-wrenching experience. If you ever really want to get your adrenaline pumping, drive one of those leviathans in heavy, fast-moving traffic, in a narrow wet lane. Then get broadsided by a strong gust of wind. Though I'd experienced that frightful sensation a few times before, what Solace and I were about to get into made being blown into another traffic lane seem like a laughable inconvenience.

We were rolling along about seventy miles north of that wild-and-wooly Houston loop. I remember locations, as well as times and dates, because I'd kept a log ever since Elaina and I bought the RV in Jersey. My thinking was, if anything happened to us--and later me--it could aid law enforcement in their inevitable investigation.

At any rate, when Solace and I were about ten miles north of Huntsville, she started acting very antsy. She kept standing up in her seat—taking a couple of semi-circular steps—plopping back down—then doing it all over again. She did the same thing whenever she had to relieve herself, but I knew that wasn't it since she'd recently emptied out. Her ears were now pointed straight up and her tail straight down. I knew her unsettled feeling was instinctual; her natural defenses telling her to take cover. I was sure it had something to do with the approaching abysmal weather.

Dark as the afternoon sky had been it suddenly became far worse. Growing quickly, on the horizon, was an ink-blue wall of doom that would soon own the entire sky. It looked impenetrable. Shocking frenetic bolts of white lightning started networking all across it, and a wind I can only describe as explosive slammed head-on into the camper. In the snap of a finger I felt like a man trying to climb a mountainous ocean wave in an underpowered dinghy.

With fingertips as sweaty as my palms, I hastily adjusted the rearview; then I checked the other two mirrors. Mine was the only vehicle in sight. It was as if everybody on the planet but me had been alerted of this horrendous impending weather.

"Hold on, sweety," I said to Solace, "we'll get out of this mess somehow."

But I had no idea how. There wasn't an exit in sight, and in a matter of minutes we'd be smack in the middle of this dark, evil tempest.

Then the situation got worse. A string of unattached clouds, black clouds, started dancing in front of that evil-blue, malignant

93

backdrop. With leg-like appendages forming instantaneously, they started dancing like angry tribal warriors. They were huge, and they were malevolent. And two of them soon turned into something even more ominous.

One leg from each cloud suddenly reached for the ground. They were both formed by violent, rotating columns of air. I was heading straight towards not one but two gigantic, Texas tornados. They were bearing down on me faster than I was them.

I thought about making a U-turn. But that was out of the question with the deep dip in the highway's grassy median. The camper surely would have gotten stuck.

Then, up ahead, through the pouring rain, I saw something-- an overpass. I'd once seen a video taken by tornado survivors who'd taken refuge beneath a similar bridge.

Then I saw something else! A stranded car on the road shoulder, maybe a hundred yards ahead, on the right. The person on the driver's side had their arm stretched out the window, waving frantically.

Clicking my eyes back at the tornados before me, I watched as the two of them now merged together. The larger one drew the lesser in and seemed to pick up even more evil energy. I had the gas pedal floored but was only going about thirty miles an hour. I was close enough to the rotating behemoth now to see a cloud of flying dust and debris beneath it.

"Oh shit, what do I do? I can stop to let these people in. If I did, I probably wouldn't make it to the overpass in time. Ah crap, I don't have a damned choice!"

As I slowed to a stop alongside the snazzy, silver Mercedes the two women inside tried desperately to open its doors. They just couldn't do it. The wind coming our way was that strong. Solace was going berserk barking, howling, and whining.

"Frigging wonderful!"

I took off my cap, threw it on the console and shouldered my door open. With a thousand high-powered raindrops pelting me, all of them hard as cement, I fought my way around the front of the RV.

The woman in the driver's seat was pushing her door but couldn't get it open. Leaning back into the wind, I grabbed a hold of the wet handle and pulled for all I was worth. After what seemed like an eternity we got it open, she made it out of the car, and I told her to hang onto the camper's boarding handle with two hands. Then, glancing at the tornado almost on top of us, I rushed around to the other side of the car. After going through the same drill with the second lady, I finally got them both, and myself, inside the camper.

The frightened women fell into the sofa behind the driver's seat, and Solace only added to the chaos by barking at them now. Whether she liked the idea of having them on board or didn't, she was adding even more tension to this terrifying moment. I grabbed her by the nape of the neck, hollered, "No!" then threw the transmission into gear.

Flying leaves and rubble were now thrashing the windshield. It had become dark as night. Leaning over the outsized steering wheel, I put my nose as close to the glass as I possibly could. Though I could see even less of the overpass now, we were gaining on it. About another fifty yards. The rain was beyond torrential at this point. A good sized tree limb flew across the swath of the high beams. The two dripping wet, thirty-something blondes were on the edge of the seat behind me, and they both leaned forward so they too could see what was coming at us. When they did, one screamed out in a strong Texas accent, "OH MY GOOD GOD, SHERRY! LOOK AT THE SIZE OF THAT THING! IT"S RIGHT ON TOP OF US! IT'S GOING TO HIT US... ANY SECOND!"

Both of them were as close to a panic as we were to the tornado. I wasn't far behind, but I fought hard to keep control of my mind. Trying to bullshit myself as much as I was the women, I said over my shoulder, "Just hold on! Hang tough! In about thirty seconds I'm going to pull over, beneath that bridge. We're going to get out and... "

I was interrupted right there, when the other lady shrieked, "DO YOU HEAR WHAT I HEAR? WE'RE GONNA DIE! THIS IS IT! THIS IS THE END!"

We'd all heard it. It was almost deafening. Solace; with her hearing capability twice that of ours, was totally out of control now. It was the dreaded roar of a runaway freight train. Airborne tree branches were now slamming the camper. One shattered a plastic roof vent. Rain was coming in. The massive tornado before us was two hundred yards across--at the base. Leaning toward the camper's oversized windshield again, I could no longer see the top of this gray, burgeoning, whirling monstrosity.

A moment later I jerked the Winnebago onto the shoulder and pulled beneath the overpass. Slamming the gearshift into park, I shut off the engine. The entire camper was rocking back and forth, protesting on its springs.

"OK, come on, we've got to get out of here! I'll go out first with the dog, you follow me!"

"Are you crazy? No fucking way! We're not going out there! We wouldn't..."

"It's our only chance! Come on! When get outside climb the abutment, all the way to the top. Come on!"

With the three of us crouched over and me nearly squeezing the life out of Solace, we fought our way up the concrete abutment. The women were in front of me shrieking and wailing like a thousand grieving mothers. The roar was absolutely ear-splitting by now. We were being battered with debris. My long hair flagged skyward in the incredibly strong updraft and right before my eyes, so did both women's skirts. This vision was so glorious that, under normal conditions, even a man in mourning wouldn't have been unable to turn away. But it meant nothing now. With poor Solace being crushed in my left arm, I alternated my right palm from the behind in pink panties to the one in black, pushing, forcing each of their owners forward. When we finally reached the top, just beneath the road, they stopped screaming as all four of us pulled into the fetal position.

Nobody said anything. All of us isolated in our own thoughts and fears, we just waited. They whimpered. Maybe they prayed also. I don't know. But during the most terrifying moments of this most horrific ordeal, I had an Epiphany.

Beneath that bridge, clinging for my life alongside that Texas highway, I realized, without a doubt, that I was *not* ready to die. With all I'd been through, and all that might lie ahead, I was not ready to pack it in. The human will to survive in the face of peril can at times be a remarkable, dauntless force.

Suddenly the wind and rain began to subside; the train had moved farther down the tracks; and somewhere above our cement ceiling the sun had broken through the clouds. Solace turned toward me, and she licked my face. I rubbed her head, and one of the women behind me said, "Oh thank you, Jesus!" Neither of them had looked like the religious types, but possibly that had now changed.

After making our way back down the abutment, we all climbed into the camper. It was still standing but the front wheels had been pushed, or lifted, five feet from where I'd left them. She cranked right up, and I threw it in reverse. With still not a vehicle in sight, I put on the emergency flashers and backed up. After my guests assured me they were alright, one told the other, "Wait till *next Sunday's* luncheon! Will we have a story for the girls?"

Their car was covered with wet leaves, but other than that, it looked fine. I told them I'd go outside and open the camper's side door; it would be easier for them to climb out. After they did, and their Benz started up, they both thanked me. They reached through the now open window and shook my hand. They had called me "suh," and it was meant to be a sign of respect, but it made me feel like an old, tired lion.

As I walked away from the car the driver's ears must have still been ringing, because I heard her say something louder than she'd intended. It certainly wasn't meant for my ears when she said, "I just figured out who he is, Sherry! I knew he looked familiar! That's that guy...Rolls...Coles...no, Soles! Yeah, that's his name. He's the one who wrote that fucked up book."

97

Chapter 13

After the tornado ordeal, we backtracked to Huntsville and paid for a site at the beautiful state park there. Even before hooking up the water hose and electric, I walked around the outside of the camper and assessed the damage. There were a few hairline scratches on both sides: three tiny chips in the windshield—none in conspicuous places; one cracked plastic reflector near the back; and the broken ceiling vent. Damage from the vent was minimal--just a wet area on the carpet between the stove and kitchen sink. I solved that problem with a handheld hairdryer, and the broken vent with some good old, dollar-store duct tape I had lying around.

Cool and clear as the next morning was, I knew it would be safe to wait until reaching Dallas before replacing the vent. We made good time and were just outside the city limits in just over two hours. I wasn't looking forward to sitting around some strange waiting room while the RV was repaired, especially with Solace and her attitude possibly drawing more attention, but I had no choice. Number one; I didn't have the tools to do the job myself, and number two; I wanted to get the oil changed.

Fortunately, being a Monday, they took me right in. Of course, when I explained to the serviceman what had happened, he recommended a full inspection of the vehicle. Perfectly aware that he wanted to build the repair bill, and stubborn as I could be when I had to, I told him no thanks. Then, wanting to quash his hopes completely, I also told him (as nicely as possible) that if the entire camper was going to self-destruct within the next ten miles I didn't even want to know about it. All I wanted was the vent, the oil change, one new reflector, and the price--upfront.

I didn't like having to be so brusque, but after all, this was the twenty-first century. Most businesses were going to try to get every dime they possibly could from me. Not only that but I knew how most car dealerships worked and figured their RV cousins weren't going to be all that different. I had a mechanic neighbor back in Queens who once bragged how in one nine-hour day he "booked" and got paid for twenty-nine hours labor. I never had much to do with him after hearing that, but I did learn a valuable lesson.

There was only one customer sitting in the stark white waiting room. Being that Solace and I had a little chat before we'd gone in, and the fact that the customer was of the female gender (which sometimes pissed my partner off a wee bit less), she behaved surprisingly well. Carefully keeping her leash snug, I helped myself to the "free" coffee and powdered cream then sat down and opened up my laptop. Surprisingly, I was able to pick up someone's Wi-Fi. Not so surprisingly, there were no new emails. I was going to check and see how *Enough is Enough* was doing on the charts, but I decided to first Google Soleswatch.com. What I saw drained the blood from my face. I know that because I suddenly felt light-headed. The tracking map showed my latest sighting was in Huntsville, Texas.

Son-of-a-bitch! I thought, *of all the thankless...aaah, what's the sense. What in the hell did I expect. This world is infested with sub-humans. I risked my life trying to save theirs, and that's the thanks I get. Sure, as it turned out, they would have made it had I not picked them up, but that's not the point. Had those two been sitting in that car the tornado could have just as easily...*

My mind went on and on like that until the serviceman came to get me. When he did, and he told me the work was going to cost an extra five dollars because the price of the vent had risen, I didn't bother to argue. I just wanted out of there, out of Texas, out of this solar system.

But that wouldn't be easy. Just getting out of Dallas would be difficult enough, and I'm not only talking traffic, either. Something very peculiar happened to me--three times. Twice while on the loop going around the city and once when I first picked up I-35 north of it. Three times I had vehicles pull up to my driver's side window and keep pace with the camper for a few moments. All three kept shooting glances across their front seats at me. Each time they'd momentarily lower their heads so they could see my face, high above in the camper's window.

The first time it happened the driver was a woman. The second two were men. I made eye contact with each of them four or five times. All of them, on the last exchange or two, gave me evil looks, hateful looks as if they'd swallowed rancid lemons. The last man gave me the bird. He shook his finger at me as if he'd just scorched it and would love to bury it in my eyes. All of them sped off as soon as they got their messages across. There was a lot of money in Dallas and obviously, a lot of unhappy people.

Unnerving as it had been since I'd discovered that Soleswatch site, it now seemed more dangerous than it had, far more dangerous. I started looking into every vehicle that passed me. Constantly checking my rearview mirror to see what was coming up next, I was spending more time looking into the thing than out the windshield. Like I said, it was plenty cool out that day but I was sweating by now. It suddenly felt like there was a huge scarlet letter emblazoned on the back and both sides of the camper. Not like the "A" for adultery in Hawthorne's novel, but a T for treason. You can't begin to fathom how bad I wanted out of that Dallas traffic.

* * *

Two mornings later, Solace and I were closing in on the Rockies. We'd driven two-hundred miles and seen nothing but Kansas wheat fields. Traffic had been all but non-existent, and that certainly helped keep my paranoia at a manageable level. But I was bored to tears with all the amber waves of grain.

After counting down innumerable mile-markers, it was a huge letdown when we finally crossed the border into Colorado. It was more of the same. As far as I could see there was only that flat, soulless landscape. The celebrated mountains were nowhere to be seen. No uplifting John Denver songs played on the radio.

For at least a solid hour my eyes scoured that barren horizon. I was beginning to think the glossy travel brochures and all the other hoopla about the Rockies were hoaxes. I thought for sure Solace was sulking in her seat; thinking how full of baloney I was for promising her an entire range of mountains to pee on.

But then something appeared out of nowhere. Something I hadn't expected. I'd been thinking all along a tiny peak would eventually blip from where the sorry moonscape met the clear blue sky. I figured that hill would eventually mushroom into something far larger as we made our way closer to Denver. But the way I'd pictured it was all wrong.

What I first saw was not small. Way off in the distance a large burgeoning shape suddenly became visible. There must have been something in the atmosphere because the vision was at first obscure--like it was slowly making its way through a cloud. As long and hard as I'd been looking, I actually thought it might be a mirage. But it wasn't. It first appeared in the western sky like the obscure, white-veiled face of a most stunning bride. As we got closer the veil seemed to slowly vanish, and the mountains began to take form. Soon it looked like the mighty kingdom of heaven itself was emerging from that cloud. It was as if I was back in another age—witnessing the birth of the continental divide as it rose from a trembling earth. I now understood what a Rocky Mountain-high is. This sight was so spiritually intoxicating that I had no business driving. It had nothing to do with my equilibrium, but I just had to pull off the road and stop on its shoulder.

I shut off the engine and studied the sight before me for a while. Finally, I rose from my seat, walked to the back of the RV, and opened one of the wooden cabinets over the bed. Inside it I snapped open two Velcro straps I'd installed back in Myrtle Beach. I then removed the urn containing Elaina's remains.

After installing Solace's harness and clipping on the leash, the three of us went outside. Solace and I stood alongside the camper, on the passenger side where we couldn't be seen by the occasional passing motorist. Holding the urn close to my heart, we took in the incredible mountain-view as I said, "We're here, Elaina. We've come a long way. I am so, so sorry, honey. It never should have been this way. I would give my life in a second to get yours back. You know that, don't you?"

101

I sniffled a few times, ran the back of my hand beneath my nose then saw something very strange atop the highest peak. It was a flash, just one flash, like a reflection from a very large mirror.

"Could it be?" I wondered out loud. "No…that's crazy."

As soon as those words left my tongue there was another flash. This time I said nothing. An invasion of goose bumps tightened the flesh on my arms. A welcome chill lifted the hair on the back of my neck. My head turned itself to the side. I looked down to where Elaina should have been standing alongside me, and I could have sworn I saw her image. It was a faint image, just like when I'd first glimpsed those mountains coming out of nowhere. And it had only been there for one fleeting moment before it dissipated. I was as unsure about seeing it as I was with the direction of my life. Yet somehow, when I climbed back into that camper, I felt a little richer than when I'd stepped out. A small nostalgic smile nudged both my cheeks, and I no longer felt so alone.

* * *

The closer we got to "The Mile High City" the more grandiose the mountains became, and unfortunately, the more traffic picked up. I was glad it was the end of winter, not the summertime. I'd seen too many pictures of Denver, shot during the hot months, when there's a brown, noxious canopy looming over the city. In those photographs it looked like the same environmental disaster that shrouds Los Angeles.

I was damn glad it was a Wednesday and mid-afternoon when we reached Denver. I could only imagine what traffic would've been like had we arrived two hours later. Though I-70 was now packed with zipping and zapping, frenzied lunatics, at least they were moving. I didn't even want to think about how unnerved I would have been in bumper to bumper traffic. I could just see all the lanes stalled, me being boxed in by hateful strangers, all of them armed with spitting-mad faces and spiteful gestures. As it was, by the time I exited near the town of Golden, I'd endured two more fun-house-scary type faces.

Unlike the ones I'd encountered in Dallas, these guys were screamers. I was getting damn sick of this treatment, real fast.

Livid as I was, something else bothered me even more. It was the fear welling inside me. Yes, I was afraid of those people, and all the others I'd surely encounter in the future. But worse than that, I was beginning to fear myself even more. I was afraid of what I might do. When those last two idiots screamed I had my hand resting on the door's armrest and my finger on the power-window button. Both times I was just about to lower the window when they sped off. I was going to curse the hell out of them and see where it went from there. Surely those situations would have escalated, and I would have told them to get off the next exit. That's where it gets frightening.

Had they followed me off the interstate I, at the very least, would have reverted to the street tactics I grew up with. I may have been only a month away from turning sixty, but I still knew how to use my fists. That would have been bad enough. But I knew I was capable of far more drastic measures. Troubled as I had become, I might very well have opened the glove box and resorted to what I'd learned in the Asian jungles. I could see myself snapping. After all, these people—right here in my own country—had become my worst enemies. Forget the North Vietnamese, the Iraqis, and most of those in the hills of Afghanistan. The way I saw it, those selfish, bitter people on these highways, and the legions of others just like them, were my only real threats. They were the ones out to seize the last shreds of so many tattered American Dreams. Any one of them might jump at the chance to kill more than just my dying spirit.

At about eight o'clock that night, after some of my anger dissipated, Solace and I were hooked up in a campground near Evergreen. She was lying alongside me on the sofa as I finished recording the day's events in my journal.

One entry expressed the disappointment I'd felt not being able to go into downtown Denver. I really wanted to knock around there a little. I would have parked the camper and had a few cold ones at Charlie Brown's; where Jack Kerouac hung out during the summer of '47. I would have traced his steps up and down Larimer Street just like I did Hemingway's in Key West.

For a while, I would have hung out on the lawn of the Capitol Building. Hopefully, I could have exchanged ideas and thoughts with like-minded individuals just as Ginsberg, Cassady, Kerouac, and all the other beats had back in the day. Just like folks continued to do a generation later, in the sixties.

But none of that was possible for me. Being the marked man I was, all that was out of the question. After all, I'd been labeled "Public enemy number 1" by some. And that nasty belief was rapidly spreading across certain social circles like a ravenous wild fire in a windstorm. The insane, spiteful notion that I and my convictions were treasonous was quickly evolving into a full-blown consensus.

What did I expect? Hadn't it been decades since all my childhood beliefs and ideals had been shot to hell? Executed? Hadn't I finally realized justice and fairness no longer meant a thing? That the strength of those virtues had been slammed aside by greed, chicanery, and power? Didn't I know that the days when the good-guys in white cowboy hats always beat the bad guys in black ones were long gone? Sure I did. For thirty years I'd watched with fearful eyes as Corporate-America and their political cronies plowed down everything in their path; just like that dark, ominous Texas tornado had done two days earlier.

While wallowing in the middle of these thoughts and disappointments the cell phone chimed for the fourth time in as many months. As I fumbled with the thing I again vowed to learn how to change the ring. Every time Elaina's favorite song—All You Need Is Love—played, it made me wince.

As if it was a question I said, "Hello?"

"Hello, Tom? How are you?" It was Denise Solchow, my sweetheart of an editor.

"Oh," I said, reaching for a cigarette, "I'm as good as can be expected, I suppose. How about you? How are you doing, Denise?"

She drew a deep breath as if preparing for a long underwater swim. I could tell this wouldn't be good news even before she said in a tired, defeated voice, "Not very well, not very well at all. As a matter of fact that's why I'm calling you, Tom."

"Sure, you're calling me because I'm such a beacon of cheer. You want me to tell you my secret for making new friends I'll bet. OK, hon...all kidding aside, what's up? Anything I can help with?"

"No, no! As a matter of fact after I tell you what I have to say, I'm not so sure you'd help me if you could."

There was an uncomfortable silence. I quit fumbling with my cigarette and lit it. I would have looked out the window into the night, but the camper curtains are always closed. After taking a deeper than normal hit, I exhaled and said, "Um, hum, what's going on, Denise?"

"I've rehearsed this over and over, Tom, for three days now. I still don't have a clue as to how I should tell you this, but here goes. We've got a problem, a serious problem. Broadstreet International wants to buy our house out."

"Oh shit! Are you kidding? No! Anybody but them! They may be the biggest, but they're the most restricting bunch of clowns out there."

"Yes, I know. And that leads to a bigger problem...oh, God, I'm really hating this. Are you sitting down, Tom?"

Nooo, I'm thinking now. *No more bad news. I don't think I can handle it.* But I braced my mindset the best I could and said, "Yes, go ahead."

"The deal is all but signed, but it gets worse. Broadstreet has one last stipulation. Tom...they want to drop *Enough is Enough*. They say it doesn't fit in with the rest of their list. They also said ..."

"Forget it, Denise. You needn't go on. I get your drift."

"Please, let me finish. You should hear the rest, in case you don't already know." There was another pause and long breath before she continued, "Through no fault of your own, your book has fallen off the charts, Tom. It's no longer even in the top hundred. Franklin and Hines is the third major retailer to take it off their shelves. They did it last week, and when they did it tanked. Broadstreet, of course, is saying that's the reason they want to drop it. They say it would be a losing proposition to hold on to it."

"You and I both know that is bullshit."

"Of course we do. With Franklin and Hines dumping it now, it cannot survive in the mainstream. And just like the other two chains, they also removed it from their online list. Hell, Tom, we're sunk."

I stubbed out my cigarette, searching the bottom of the glass ashtray as I did; looking for my next words. When I finally found them I said, "I don't know why I'm so damn shocked. I knew all along that one way or another they'd get rid of it. What a shame. That book has staying power. It would have kept on selling for a long time. A lot of good things could have been accomplished with those future royalties."

"I know, Tom," Denise said, her voice beginning to crack now, "You've done some wonderful things with your money. You've helped many, many people."

"Yeah...thanks, I know. But what I've done is just a drop in society's cruel, cold, needful bucket."

"Call it what you want, but I don't think there's a soul alive who would have done what you have. And look...look what you've gotten in return. You've got to run, hide out. You've had threats on your life, and my God...poor Elaina. We both know what they did with her mold. I've never met a human being who could come..."

"I know, Denise, thank you, thank you very much," I interrupted, "but what about you? Have you run into any flack from the outside? Has anyone threatened you in any way? Anything out of the ordinary occurred in these last two years?"

"Oh, I've gotten a few calls at the office, a few emails questioning my principles, that kind of malarkey. Other than that, no, there's been nothing serious. As I've told you before, in all my years in the publishing business, I've never once handled a book that's had nearly as many positive responses as yours. There were times, before the mega-retailers dropped it, that I was inundated with calls and emails."

"Well thank God for that. So what's next? What are you going to do now? Are you willing to work for those censors-- those propagandists? Are they even going to let you?"

"Being you and I have had our relationship for two years now, I seriously doubt it. They've already told all the editors at a meeting they're going to *strengthen* the staff. You know what that means, right?"

"You bet. Heads are going to roll. They'll be bringing in their like-minded dullards."

"Everybody in the industry knows they only lean one way. I'll be the first to go."

Stroking Solaces head now I asked, "What are you going to do, Denise? What's your next move?"

"I don't know for sure. I've got a close friend at a small publishing house. I've talked to him. He seems to think they might be interested in me. I should know more by next week. I've been in this business twenty-three years, Tom. It's all I know. It's all I really want to know. But times are tough. Most publishers are culling their lists instead of adding to them."

Denise cleared her throat. Then, in a voice laced with hundred-proof, genuine concern, she said, "All right, enough about me. What about you, Tom? How are you holding up? I don't want to rub salt in any wounds, but my God, how are you getting by with all that's happened?"

I filled her in about Soleswatch.com and a few of the incidents that had occurred, but that was it. I didn't want to overload her with my problems. She had enough liver on her own plate.

She did give me a bit of encouragement that took some of the sting out of all the bad news. She said she was confident that, if she landed an editor's position at her friend's place, there was a good chance they'd pick up *Enough is Enough*. The downside was, if they did publish it, they'd probably only do so in paperback.

She also told me, considering the bind I was in, she'd fully understand if I didn't think such a move would be prudent. As the conversation drew to a close, she asked if I thought I'd want to put the book back onto store shelves; would it be worth the risk. My answer was a resounding, "Hell Yes!"

Chapter 14

At five AM the next morning, it was as dark and still inside the camper as it was outside in the Rocky Mountain foothills. As always, no matter where we were at first squint, Solace the bed hog had me pinned to the mattress edge. Slowly reentering the here and now, my first thoughts were the same ones I'd taken to bed—my finances. With the book being thrown out by yet another mega-retailer and Broadstreet International dumping it, it was time to get serious about tightening my budget. With my dreaded sixtieth birthday still three weeks away, I still had two more years before being eligible for my social security pittance. Even with my usual monk-like spending habits, I'd need twice what that "security net" was going to pay.

Elaina and I had always squeezed every penny we spent. For as long as I could remember, we'd been tearing paper towels in half; using them twice when possible. We were always one-light-on-at-a-time folks, and many years ago, I cut two pieces from a foam rubber doormat to fit inside my bargain basement sneakers. To this very day, I still put them inside my footwear every time the inner soles lose their cushion. All I wear on my back are those four-dollar tees or sweatshirts that don't cost much more. Sure, I had a dress shirt or two for special occasions. But I've always had trouble fighting back a wry smile whenever I saw another man with one of those cutesy little logos embodied over his heart. Knowing he'd paid three times what I had for a very similar shirt, and that he believed it to be an all-important status symbol, time and again made it hard for me to keep a straight face.

We'd always clipped coupons and loaded up on sale items—even before mayonnaise went up to five dollars a jar—a plastic jar at that. As for those rebate doohickeys hardly anybody bothers with, Elaina always made damn sure she sent them in before they expired. If the supermarket was out of the generic mustard, laundry detergent, pink salmon or whatever, we would never pay more for the name brands. We'd do without because we knew well and good that "shrinking inventories" is no accident. Often, the stores we shopped would be out of a product two, three weeks straight so that customers would *have* to shell out more for the expensive brands.

Yes, lying in bed that early morning I knew it was time to plan a strategy. With my future royalties on the verge of disappearing, I had to figure out how much money I'd need behind me to get through whatever was ahead of me. Before making my next donation to charity, I had to figure out how much I'd need to subsist on. That would not be easy because I didn't know if I'd be above the dirt for another two hours or twenty-five years.

The decision to buy a small place in Maine had already been made. That was a done deal. A little later, after my jog and coffee, I decided I had to get rid of the New York apartment. Financially the decision was easy; emotionally it was a killer. I'd lived there almost forty-four years and was as comfortable as an old squirrel in his favorite tree. I knew every neighbor, shop-owner, and alleyway shortcut. But once I called Manny Ruiz and cancelled the lease there'd be no going back. Because it was a "rent-controlled" building, and I'd been there so long, I'd never again get a place for a third of what I'd been paying. If by some chance I happened to have a future, it would not be in New York. It *could* not be. And that hurt deeply. I'd now arrived at a point where I'd not only lost my wife and my freedom, but I was about to lose my past as well.

You see, in many ways, the place where you grow up is like a lover. You can leave that place or you can stay in it. You can love it more as time passes, or you can come to hate it. You can be proud of it and sometimes, not so proud of it. If you leave a place, the memories you take with you may be fond, tragic or anywhere in between. But one thing is for sure, unlike discarded lovers, there is no divorcing the place you called home. That place will be with you wherever you venture. It will always be an integral part of you. And at some point in your life, it will beckon your return.

The place where I became most of who I am was not beautiful. There were no rolling verdant hills. No pastures, forests, lakes or streams. The sky, what I could see of it, was often gray. The people there didn't say hello to strangers--they were wary of them. But none of that mattered. I still felt the incessant pull of "home." I knew that if I survived, I would someday submit to that pull, even if for just a short visit.

Solace's sudden barks, followed by a sharp knock at the camper's door, yanked me out of my ruminations. Looking out the window, I saw the same strictly-business, forty-something redhead who'd checked me in at the office the afternoon before. She'd reminded me of a short Lucille Ball in a cowboy shirt. Since she was still wearing it at eight in the morning I assumed she was the owner, putting in long hours.

"Just a minute," I said as I grabbed a hold of Solace and whisked her off to the bedroom. "I'll be right there."

"Yes," I said a moment later, after opening the door.

"Mister Frances, I just received a very strange phone call," she said as if she'd just caught me breaking six of the campground's most hallowed rules.

"Okayyy," I said, pushing my hair back from my eyes.

"Someone, some strange sounding man, called and said I should give you a message. He said to give it to *Thomas Soles* in site 6-B. I knew I should have checked your driver's license."

"Hold on, I can exp…"

"I don't want you explaining anything," she ranted, "just take this damn message and get out of here. I don't know who the hell you really are or what you're into, but I don't want your kind around here. I'll give you thirty minutes, that's it. Within thirty minutes you're outta here," then she yanked her tiny thumb."

"But I…"

"Forget it, buster, if you're not gone, I call the sheriff. As a matter of fact, I think I'll call them anyway…right now. Take this goddamn thing."

I took the envelope; she spun out of there, leaving small clouds of arrogant dust with her boots.

Back in the camper, I didn't even sit down. Solace was still going crazy in the bedroom, but she could wait a minute. With adrenaline-fuelled, shaky hands I opened the white envelope. The message was short and to the point. It said, "If you're still there at sunset, Soles, you and your dog won't be around to see midnight. Leave Colorado now! You sorry son-of-a-bitch."

With Solace still barking in the background, I shot right out the camper door to disconnect the hookups. I yanked the plug from the site's power source and hastily stuffed the cord into its outside storage compartment. As I hurriedly unscrewed the water hose, my eyes clicked from one direction to the next. I hadn't yet opened the awning, so there would be no need to screw with that. I dashed back inside; let Solace out of the bedroom and double-checked Elaina's ashes. The Velcro was secured. I chucked the ashtray and my coffee cup in the sink and made sure everything else had been secured.

I did all that in less than five minutes. I also took the Glock out and placed it on the console, within reach. Then I pulled out of that site so fast, I forgot there was a dip where it met the unpaved road. When my front wheels bounced in and out of the depression, I heard a loud, disheartening crunch. I flung it in park, raced around the camper and saw that, in my haste, I'd forgotten to raise the side door's metal entry steps. The bottom step was creased in the center, but luckily, I was still able to fold them up.

Crazed as I was, my forehead furrowed deep as plowed rows, I rushed out of there, casting hateful, suspicious stares at every camper I saw. When I reached the campground's open gates, I fired up a smoke and headed toward the highway. It wasn't easy, but I held back and forced myself not to speed.

Who knows, maybe there was no message. Maybe she made the whole thing up. Maybe it took her a while to realize who I am, and when she did she concocted this scheme. Maybe that's bullshit, and some head case really did leave the message. Maybe he was dead serious. Maybe he actually was going to try to kill me. Maybe he figured he'd be better off waiting till after dark. I don't know if he was a camper staying at the park or he followed me in there. Either way, he knew exactly which site I was in. He called in that threat. Who knows what somebody like that is capable of? My God, there are thousands just like him

111

out there. Probably tens of thousands! I'm sure more than a few are nut jobs who'd jump at the chance to put a bullet in my head. Fifteen-thousand murders a year in this dumbed-down, berserk country. My God...what do I do now?

With that last question center-stage to all the others jamming my mind, my eyes shifted from the windshield to the pistol on the console. I realized then and there that I had no choice; wherever I went I'd have to start wearing my shirt outside my pants. I was not going to wait for death or accept it peacefully.

Chapter 15

Fighting valiantly to maintain a semblance of composure, I headed north on Interstate 25. I mean, how much could one human being take? Just three years earlier, I could have been the poster boy for this country's obscure masses. An inconsequential doorman from Queens, New York, I had about as much notoriety as a discarded cigarette butt smoldering outside a rush hour subway entrance.

Would I, you might ask, have still written the book had I'd known my life was going to devolve into such a hellish existence? You may think I'm farther over the top than I really am, but even as I was high-tailing it out of Denver, I would have said yes. I'm one of those fools who would die for their principles. I hate more than anything living in a world full of half-truths and lies. No citizen or society should be subject to that. But the only way I'd write that book again, is if I knew Elaina would remain alive, and only if she agreed to it. Sure, if she said yes, and I knew what I did now, I would have handled things differently. I'd have taken her straight to Maine. We'd have bought that little place deep in the North Woods and hopefully grown old together.

Tragically, it was too late for twenty-twenty hindsight. Nothing could bring Elaina back. All I could do at this point was try to keep myself alive, and that wasn't going to be easy. It seemed everyone in America with a stock portfolio or hundred-thousand-dollar income had their sights set on me. But ironic as it is, what scared me even more than those barracudas were the Soles-haters who'd never had an extra twenty bucks in their lives. The same poor unfortunates who'd been brainwashed since first learning the Pledge of Allegiance were the ones who worried me most. And to think they were the exploited, neglected unfortunates I'd most wanted to help. Unfortunately, they were, and still are as I write this, part of the growing, misinformed herd that's constantly bamboozled by hokey, TV-propaganda machines, masquerading themselves as "news shows."

Before making it out of Denver that harried morning, I encountered yet another of those misguided souls. A big, burly Bubba type driving a beat pickup with a serious muffler problem pulled alongside me. With my window closed and the racket his truck made, I couldn't hear what he was yelling, but I sure could read his lips. What he said wasn't pretty, neither was the plump, wingless bird he kept pumping at me.

Still, this frazzled, moving target pushed his Winnebago north—at speeds that would have earned me a reckless-endangerment charge, had I been caught. With all the panic-induced clutter pinging inside my head, I wasn't thinking of the possible consequences. I just wanted out of there. Had my mind been coherent I might have envisioned the very real possibility of being thrown in some small town pokey--with an angry mob and plenty of tar and feathers waiting outside for my release. But that didn't enter my mind. All I knew was I wanted to keep driving. It was the only thing that made any sense.

After clearing out of Denver, Solace and I made it over the Wyoming border in less than sixty minutes. I not only logged eighty miles that hour, but shot hundreds of backward glances as well. My eyes constantly ricocheted from one rearview mirror to the next. If it had been possible to transform fear into heat, the terror in my eyes would have shattered or melted all three of them.

I was living in, no, *fleeing in* a combat zone where the enemy wore no uniform. Any adversary with killing on his mind could simply walk up to me and fulfill his mission. Sneaking up would not be necessary. With no way of identifying him, and my inability to read dangerous thoughts, I was an easy bull's-eye for any overzealous vigilante that happened along. The end could come at any time; while I was driving; filling my gas tank; walking Solace; stocking up on groceries; even sleeping. It was much the same feeling as patrolling a tree line in Viet Nam. Over there I never knew if or when a sniper's bullet might find me. Now, here in my own country, I was carrying that same frightful dread. As I write this, it still weighs heavy on me.

As we made our way across Wyoming and Montana the next two days, I calmed down somewhat, allowing my frayed defense mechanisms a well-deserved respite. You see, in both those states, you can drive one, two, three-hundred miles and more between sizable towns. And each time we made our way across one of those seemingly-endless stretches; I actually slowed down rather than sped up. With traffic all but nonexistent, I wanted to savor every mile of this most welcome solitude. If I was going to hold onto what was left of my sanity, I needed those extended opportunities. Each long, straight, solitary road was yet another chance to simmer my anxiety and heal my perspective. It didn't matter whether the landscape was a flat, desolate prairie or an absolutely astonishing, chills-up-the-spine mountain range, I took my time. And that's why, at the end of that second day, it was already dark out when Solace and I neared our final destination in Western Montana.

At about seven o'clock I exited the highway for a pit stop in Missoula. I needed a pack of Carlton cigarettes, and Solace needed to relieve herself. A lighted digital sign outside a bank on Broadway Street flashed a temperature reading of twenty-seven degrees. Missoula had a population of 62,000; but on this night, it seemed most folks were at home, cozying up in front of their woodstoves and fireplaces. There was nary a soul in sight. A faint dash of fine snow breezed through a streetlight's glow, as I pulled the camper alongside a convenience store. After I ran inside and Solace took care of her business, overtired as we both were, we slogged right back onto I-90.

I didn't know that a nearby campground was actually open year-round, but I darned well did know I was nowhere near ready to check into a motel. All I wanted at this point was to find a quiet place--outside of town--where I could pull over for the night. Cold as it was, I knew Solace and I would do just fine with the camper's propane heater working as well as it had been.

About forty minutes later, I pulled off an exit that put us smack in the middle of Lolo National Forest. There I followed a dark, deserted road that plowed deeper and deeper into an eternity of towering pines. Fifteen minutes passed and I hadn't seen the lights of a car, truck, house or anything. The Bitterroot Mountain Range and the Idaho border were close by, but I couldn't see a thing other than the road in my headlights and the black trees engulfing me. Exhausted as I was, out there in the middle of nowhere, I could not find a single place to pull over. With the trees so close to the road, there wasn't even a shoulder to park on.

Finally, after crossing over what looked like a narrow river, I saw a possibility. There was a small clearing to the right of the road, surely where fishermen had parked their vehicles. Of course, it was empty now.

I hit the brakes after passing it, backed up slowly, then got out and accessed the area. As I backed further into it, I had to get out three more times to make sure the camper didn't wind up in the shallow river. One quick cigarette later, Solace and I went to bed. In no time at all, we were both in a deep sleep, so deep that neither of us heard the pickup truck stop in front of the camper.

A sharp rap at the door awoke us. Tired as she was, Solace immediately went into one of her high-pitched, terrier barking fits; and she sprung out of bed. Still dressed in my driving clothes, I rushed to the front, grabbed the pistol. Slowly pushing aside a living room curtain with one finger, I peered out with one eye.

The intruder was standing in front of the side door. From my high perch inside the camper, I couldn't make out his face. Looking down the way I was, I could only see the top of a wide-brimmed cowboy hat--a black cowboy hat at that.

Solace was attacking the door, barking, scratching--just going plain loco.

Three more raps at the door. It may have been pitch black outside, but I was now close enough to see that the knocks were being made with the business end of a shotgun.

"Yeah?" I finally said in a tone as firm and deep as I could muster, "What do you want?"

Then, in a tone not nearly as deep as mine but just as firm, the intruder said, "What I want is you off my property, right now. What gives you the right to..."

Now realizing the gun-toting culprit was a woman I shouted above Solace's barking, "Give me a minute! Let me put the dog away!"

After wrestling Solace into the bedroom and closing the door, I flipped on the outside light and opened the entry door.

Then, with an intonation that was still less than friendly I said, "Look..." but before continuing my verbal defense I was forced to do just that—look.

Standing out there in the cold, beneath that black Stetson, was one of the most striking faces ever to grace my eyes. Just looking at her would make any red-blooded cowboy howl like a coyote. Whether he was a rodeo cowboy, an urban cowboy, a space cowboy, or even a garden-variety vegetarian there'd be no looking away.

She was not a young woman; probably in her late forties, but maturity had yet to lay claim to her rare beauty. If anything, all the dawns and dusks she'd witnessed may have actually added to her appeal. Her sleek, no-nonsense eyes didn't ask for my attention, they demanded it. They were dark, every bit as dark as the long hair she'd stuffed beneath her coat collar. The coat itself was really a heavy jacket, and what it revealed below her waist—wrapped tight in faded blue jeans—would have made women half her age jealous and kept all those cowboys a howling.

Her shotgun was now pointed down, but with the stock under her arm and a finger on the trigger it was still at the ready. She was visibly perturbed and breathing quite heavily. Angry streams of mist flowed from her cold, delicate nostrils as well as her mouth. She didn't say a thing. She just stared me down like a cross school teacher would a defiant student.

"Look...I'm sorry," I said, switching the tone of my appeal to a more diplomatic one, "but I've been on the road for five days. I thought it would be easy to find a place out here where I could spend the night. But it wasn't. I was almost falling asleep at the wheel and..."

Now it was her turn to interrupt. "Whoooa, hold on, wait a minute! I know who you are!"

Here it comes, I thought, sliding my finger on the trigger behind my back. *I don't want to do this! Especially to a woman, for God's sake!*

"You're Thomas Soles, for crying out loud! Sure...the New York plate, the camper, you're him!"

"Yes...you're right. I am Thomas Soles. So what's next?" I said, nodding at her shotgun.

She looked at it as if it she'd forgotten it was there. I watched intently. But when her eyes met mine again, her gorgeous face suddenly was awash with sympathy.

"My Lord, you don't look so hot, nothing like you do on TV or your book jacket."

"Yes, I know," I said, pushing my hair back. "So, you've seen my book? Did you burn it, too?"

"Are you kidding? There may not be many people around these parts who think like *you* do, but I sure as hell do. I'm one of your biggest fans."

With Solace still raising holy hell in the bedroom, the woman glanced side to side, up and down the dark road. Then, tilting her felt hat back just a bit, she looked at me like a caring mother would at a deeply troubled child.

Her voice then became secretive and concerned, but there was also a hint of excitement in it. "You *cannot* stay out here-- next to the road. Sean Gerrity, the deputy sheriff, patrols it. He comes by few times every night. He's a nice enough guy, but nobody around here is all too fond of strangers. Follow me. My driveway's just ahead. Nobody will bother you there. You can park on either side of my cabin."

With the palm of my free hand, I smoothed the hair on the back of my head a couple of times then said, "Nooo, I appreciate the gesture, but I can't..."

"Oh stop! Don't be silly! After reading *Enough is Enough,* I feel like I already know you." Then, without budging her eyes from mine, she paused, pointed to the barrel of her gun, wagged it twice and said, "Besides, I'm certainly not worried."

Then, ever so slowly, her lips evolved into a small, warm smile. Somehow, all at once, this gentle pull of feminine lips was as mischievous as it was soothing, innocuous as it was evocative. I felt like I'd known this smile all my life but was now seeing it for the first time. Something stirred deep inside me--an irrepressible, primordial sense of attraction, and I hated myself for it.

My gut told me I should decline her offer, thank her, slam the door closed, crank up the engine, and flee into the lonely Montana night. But I didn't. Feeling overly guilty; hedonistic, like an adulterer about to cross that forbidden line, I said, "Sure. Okay. Thank you very much. We won't be any trouble. I promise my dog will calm down soon as we get settled in. And we'll be out of your hair at first light."

Still wearing that mesmerizing smile, she said, "No need for that. Folks around here say I make some wicked-good pancakes. I'll have the batter ready by seven."

"No, noo, nooo, I don't want you to..."

"Yes, yes, yes. I insist. I want to get *something* out of this deal. I'd love to be able to talk to Thomas Soles for an hour or so."

Unable to fight back a weary smile, I said, "Okay, but just an hour. Solace and I'll have to be moving on."

As soon as I said that, her smile shrunk a bit. I thought I saw a hint of disappointment in her eyes and her face as well. But still, she extended her hand and said, "I'm Julie...Julie Dubois."

I followed the red taillights of her pickup down a long dirt driveway. When we got to the end, I turned around in a spacious clearing and backed the camper alongside Julie Dubois' log A-frame. After that, she gave me a small wave; then disappeared inside her cabin.

Exhausted as I was, I did not sleep well that night. I tossed and turned so much that Solace eventually abandoned me for the living room sofa.

Chapter 16

I didn't fall into the welcome arms of sleep until the wee hours that night. So late was it that my ever-reliable, built-in reveille horn sounded an hour later than usual. What little sleep I did get was fitful, yet somehow my return to consciousness wasn't the same dawdling process it usually was. Stretched out on the empty bed for the first time in many weeks, my eyes snapped to attention as if I'd caught myself dozing at the wheel. Still black as pitch in the camper and outside, my mind lit up like a theater at the end of a movie. My renegade first thoughts were the same ones that had kept me awake. They were of Julie Dubois, and I did not like them.

Again, one side of my brain pleaded with me to start the engine and head for the hills. The other had conflicting thoughts. It said, no, you can't do that. You told this woman, who was kind enough to invite you here, that you'd simply have breakfast with her. Then you'd leave. That's it. No big thing. But on the other hand, she *is* one of the most beautiful women you've ever seen. And she seemed to take a liking to you.

"Nooo, she did not," I said aloud. "She was just being friendly…no, not friendly, I mean…hospitable."

Now overhearing my soliloquy, Solace jumped off the sofa and padded into the bedroom. After putting up with a few of her usual morning face licks, I petted her head, gave her a few pats on the side, and said, "Okay, sweetie. I'll take you out in a minute."

There was something I absolutely had to do first.

The room was chilly and so were my ears, but I forced myself out from beneath the comforter. I opened the overhead cabinet and rested my hands on the brass urn. It was cold to the touch. I wanted to warm it. Massaging its curves as if they were Elaina's, I closed my eyes. I saw my wife, and I whispered to her, "God, how I miss you, Elaina. I love you so much. I always will. I promise you…there will never be anyone else."

But how can anybody, man or woman, make such a promise? How can we be sure there will never be anybody else? After all, we are *only* human beings. We're just cells and tissue and flawed by nature. Who knows for sure what we're capable of? As time slowly heals us, as the months and years distance us from the initial paralyzing loss of a soul mate, are we supposed to move on? Or is it mandatory that, for the rest of our lives, we fight back our innate need for companionship? Is it possible the first person we loved was the only one on the planet we are capable of loving? Who's to say?

Those were the questions I asked myself, as I waited in the dark morning for Solace to do her business. But I had no answers, and I felt I had no moral right looking for them. Not the least bit too soon I gave myself a mental reprimand.

You fool, I thought, *you ARE losing your mind aren't you? Elaina's only gone four months, and you've got the gall, the cold-hearted audacity to think of another woman. What kind of low-life are you? You spend five minutes talking to somebody and you're entertaining thoughts of a future with her? Five minutes! Whoosh, you are crazy. Who says she'd even be interested? There you go again! Forget about her. Mourn for your wife, idiot. Stop acting like a schoolboy with his first crush. Solace is done now. Take her inside, clean up, go eat the damned breakfast, and get your ass out of here.*

That was the plan when I again stepped out of the camper an hour later. Gobble down those pancakes, have one cup of coffee, answer a few questions then leave. It was almost as if I was mad at Julie Dubois, like I resented her. After all the thoughts and reservations that played havoc with my head that night, my mind was as wrung out as my body. I did not want to deal with this woman. But there was no other way. When I closed the camper's door behind me, I felt the same bittersweet feeling a young boy does when he forces his first date on himself.

With the new day announcing its arrival, I made my way up the alley between the Winnebago and the log cabin. Close enough to smell the pine walls and the smoke from the chimney I glanced at a curtained window. A light inside made the blue fabric glow. A few steps later, as I cleared the front bumper, I got my first glimpse of Julie Dubois' landscape. No, I should say it was my first glimpse of God's landscape, because it had to be some of his finest work.

As if it were bashful, dawn's first light blushed pink on the eastern horizon, silhouetting the tree tops of an endless pine forest. Closer in, at the end of the spacious clearing, I saw the same river I'd seen by that bridge the night before. High above it, two bald eagles glided side by side on straight wings. One of the majestic birds let out a loud creaking cackle as they both scanned the moving water for breakfast.

To the west, on my right side, the Bitterroot Mountains towered high above like a tree-covered cloud. With only a half mile of flat land separating the cabin from this massive wall, I had to tilt my head back, way back, to see its snowy peaks. These mountains were huge and made me feel small, yet they were not imposing. Instead, they seemed protective. Studying them in awe, I felt as though nothing harmful could ever come from the far side of them.

Fifty yards in front of where I stood, the same road I'd come in on the night before cut its way through lofty pines and spruce trees. I took one long breath, marched to the cabin door, then knocked.

I hadn't thought it possible, but she was even more attractive than the night before. Not quite as tall, without the hat, she was still average height. And her hair, well, if hair alone could ever be considered evocative, hers was. Carefully brushed to the waist, it was so black, so satiny, that had it been dark I would have seen the fireplace's orange flames dancing in it. But striking as her hair was, the real showpiece was framed by it. The way her hair laid so dark and elegant behind her cheekbones, it enhanced her captivating face and all the drama in those dark eyes. But there was more to this visual feast. Packed tight in a pink western shirt and blue jeans, the curves and swells of her body were so voluptuous they could have brought a dead man back to life. With her beauty and sensual delights, it was obvious this was a woman who'd been breaking hearts and launching lovesick fantasies all her life. As she

122

looked at me and smiled in that open doorway I didn't think I'd be able to speak. Yes, she was that astonishing.

"Well, good morning Mister Soles," she said, gently nudging a gray cat back inside with a dainty cowboy booted foot, "Come on in."

"Good morning to you, Julie, and please, call me Tom," I said, crossing the threshold along with all my self-consciousness, "Say, this is a really neat little place. I had no idea from the outside it could be so roomy."

"Why thanks. It's only this room, a small bedroom in back, and the loft above it, but it's all me and my three cats need. Since it's an A-frame, with such a high ceiling, it feels far more spacious than it really is. Come," she said sweeping an arm toward a southwestern style sofa in the middle of the room, "have a seat. Coffee?"

"Sure, that sounds great. Cream only, if you have it."

As she rustled up the cups and poured coffee a few steps away in the little kitchen area, I glanced around her place. There was a colorful totem pole area rug at my feet and a wooden coffee table on top of it. On the same wall as the kitchen, but back about ten feet, was the crackling fireplace. On the opposite side of the room, there was a sprawling, well-stocked bookcase. She had a small TV, but the way it was tucked off to the side, I could tell it didn't get much use. On the walls, were a few western motif pictures; an American Indian blanket; a large, powder-blue dream-catcher; and two windows with the curtains drawn. Had they been open and my camper not parked where it was, I'd have been able to see the river and the sun coming up beyond it. To the right of where I sat, through a large picture window, the view of the mountains was beyond the words I previously attempted to describe them with. Looking out at them in the early morning light, actually made *me* feel lucky to be alive. But that sense of well being didn't last. I quickly shoved it aside and replaced it with guilt and sorrow. Lord, how I wished Elaina had been looking out that window with me.

"Here we go," Julie said, handing me a steamy cup, jerking me back into reality.

"I was just admiring this view, Julie. You're a lucky lady to see such a vision outside your window every day."

"Yes," she said, as she sat in a chair on the opposite side of the area rug and table, "I'm really lucky." But I could tell her heart wasn't in her words. They seemed laced with nostalgia and disappointment. It seemed we just might have something in common.

Then, suddenly perking up, she said, "Well, how did you sleep, Tom?"

"Good, good," I lied, "I feel a whole lot better than last night."

"That's good. I'm sure you can use all the rest you can get."

"Do I look that bad?"

"Oh, I'm sorry. I didn't mean it that way. It's just that...well, you know, you've been in the news an awful lot since you were awarded the Nobel Prize. And I keep abreast of..."

Seeing her becoming uncomfortable now, I interrupted, "I'll bet you never dreamed you'd be having coffee, here in your place, with me."

"No I certainly didn't."

Keeping her eyes on mine, she then took a sip of coffee.

Seizing the chance to change the subject I said, "What do you do, Julie? I mean for a livelihood. Do you work?"

"Yes, but to me it really isn't work. Mondays and Wednesdays I teach a few classes in Missoula, at the University of Montana."

"No kidding. What do you teach?"

"Take a guess."

"I haven't got much to go on but if I had to guess, from the looks of all those books over there," I said brushing them with my eyes, "I'd say it had something to do with literature."

"Bravo. You're right. I teach English Literature. I used to teach full time, back in New Hampshire where I'm from, but why I left, that is a...well, it's a long story with an unhappy ending. Nobody likes those. Hey, how's your coffee holding up?

We talked like that all through breakfast, exchanging pleasantries and bits of background information. As Julie had alluded the night before, her pancakes were "wicked-good." At first it felt awkward, not to mention taboo, being alone with a woman-- particularly this woman, but in no time at all, the light-hearted banter flowed free and easy.

After we moved back to the sofa and chair for a second round of coffee, we traded thoughts about some of the novels we'd both read. I talked a little about growing up in New York. She shared a few memories from her girlhood in New England. She also asked what it was like in Stockholm, when I received the prize, and I tried my best to explain the feeling.

I'd never felt any great attraction to cats before, but all three of hers hung around us humans the entire time, and they were remarkably friendly. Two made themselves at home on my lap, and I stroked them as we talked. For the first time in ages, I was actually enjoying myself. This was a sorely-needed, soothing respite from the paranoiac bars I'd been living behind. But when Julie said she'd love to meet my dog and asked what her name was, that peaceful easy feeling quickly deflated.

"Her name's Solace," I said, "I picked her up at an animal shelter in South Carolina three months ago." Then I slipped and said, "I was tired of being alone."

Julie shifted in her chair and her face grimaced slightly, as if she'd been pinched. It was obvious she felt bad for me and wanted to see inside my soul. Instead of just looking into my eyes, she was now trying to see *through* them. Fishing for more information she asked, "Did you name her Solace or did the previous owners?"

Beginning to feel cornered now, I said, "Well, yes...I did."

"Well, Solace is a nice name...unusual, but nice."

Then there was a silence. I picked my cup up from the table and looked inside it. The only audible sounds were the snapping and popping in the fireplace. Suddenly it seemed louder. I wished I'd left after the damn pancakes.

Looking back at her I said, "Look, thanks for the..."

"I'm sorry, Tom." she interrupted, in a gentle voice. "I'm so very sorry for what happened to Elaina."

That was it. She meant well, but she'd entered hallowed ground. I put the coffee cup back on the table, lowered both the cats to the floor and stood up.

"Don't leave, Tom." she said, rising to her feet now. "Please, stay a little longer. That was foolish of me. I don't know you well enough to..."

"No, that's okay. Certainly you meant no harm. I know what you were trying to do, and it was very thoughtful. I've just got to be...I just have to get going."

I then walked over to her and put out my hand. I felt the gesture was necessary. Short as our time together had been, I could already tell that this woman was an exceptionally warm and caring human being. I even laid my other hand on top of hers as we gently grasped hands. I say grasped because we did not shake.

As she walked me to the door, I said to the cats at my feet, "Bye guys." Then I opened the door and turned back around. Looking down into Julie Dubois' warm eyes, I said, "Thanks so much for the breakfast and for letting me stay last night. That was very, very kind of you."

I managed a heartfelt smile, but it did not last. It faded as she lifted her hand toward my face. Softly, she brushed the hair back from my forehead and said, "Stay safe, Tom. You didn't deserve any of what's happened to you. You're a good man."

I just stood there for a moment, slowly nodding my head. Then I turned around and left.

Chapter 17

Lumbering away from the cabin in the camper, I couldn't help but to keep checking the rearview mirror. Julie's door did not open. She did not wave me back. I wouldn't have known how to react if she had. The only thing that did move was the thin stream of smoke rising from her chimney and two horses in front of a small stable that I hadn't seen before. Once the cabin was out of sight, I realized how stupid of me it was to think a woman like her might try to prevent me from leaving. Even if she had wanted to, I could tell Julie Dubois had far too much class and empathy to do such a thing.

Picking up speed towards Missoula, looking for a campground, I kept thinking about how she'd caressed my hair to the side. Being the emotional sort I am, that small, sympathetic gesture moved me deeply. It told me everything I needed to know about this woman. Had this been another time, under different conditions, she'd have had to pull out that shotgun to get rid of me.

Sure, I'd only known her for an hour, but there is no requisite waiting period when it comes to human magnetism. Attraction, appeal, charisma, chemistry, whatever you want to label it, has moods and methods all of its own. And when it pulls, the instinctual feeling is undeniable. This joining of souls and desires can be an evolutionary process, taking years to come to fruition. But it can also strike in an instant. A man and woman may be standing at adjoining checkout lanes at a supermarket and witlessly make eye contact. Their glances could linger for just a second or two longer than usual, but that is enough. Because of this random crossing of visual paths, they share an unexpected strong yearning. There's heat in their eyes, and they both feel it. Neither says anything because it may not be what people deem "appropriate." But the following week they both feel a compulsion to do their shopping at the exact same time. Maybe they meet again; maybe they don't, but that rare attraction was there. A most profound human phenomenon had occurred and they both knew it. If their eyes never do meet again, both may be very surprised by how long a profound sense of loss continues to linger.

Yes, that was how I felt about this Julie Dubois. To let such a woman slip away seemed a crime, a sad, unfortunate crime. But I couldn't help it. The timing just wasn't right. Again, I was nowhere near ready for a romantic relationship. Yet somehow, emotionally crippled as I was, another sense of loss had now found its way into my ailing heart.

Not wanting to be a sitting duck, or a rolling one, I really didn't want to go into downtown Missoula. But there was no other choice. Without access to Wi-Fi it would have been doubly difficult to find a local campground open in mid-March. So Solace and I rolled into the parking lot of a Holiday Inn, parked in back, and were able to get online. After locating the RV park that was open year round, I jotted down the directions from MapQuest and drove out there.

The campground offered limited services during the offseason but that was fine by me. With average high temperatures in the forties, we wouldn't be spending a whole lot of time outdoors; all I wanted was a place to hole up for a month or so, before heading to Maine. I pretty much had my choice of sites and as always, chose the most secluded one. It had one beautiful mountain view. As I looked through an opening in the surrounding trees, it put me to mind of one of those calendar photographs.

After setting up and taking my sidekick for a stroll, I put on some more coffee and turned on the laptop. The same five pictures of me were on Soleswatch--three with a beard and two without. Anybody who'd seen them would recognize me either way. Convinced now that I looked better without it and ten years younger, I decided to shave it off later that day. I'd keep the moustache, but the rest would go. I then tormented myself a little for suddenly becoming vain after meeting Julie Dubois, but I was steadfast and kept denying it.

The Soleswatch map was both good and bad news. I had been spotted after leaving Dallas, but the last sighting was in Casper, Wyoming. At least, for now, nobody knew I was here.

When I'd checked into the campground, the teenager in the office seemed preoccupied and didn't ask for my driver's license, so I was able to give him another counterfeit name. Wanting to try the place out before locking in for a month, I paid for three days, with cash, of course. When I left the office, I could have kicked myself. Who was to say that, if I extended my stay as planned, there wouldn't be a by-the-book-clerk who'd want to fill out all new paperwork and see my license?

For the next three mornings, after my jog, I stopped into the park office for a cup of their free coffee. Unfortunately, every time the same lady was there. She was a strictly business, no nonsense, no personality, not even a hello, older woman in her seventies. Don't get me wrong, with my cap pulled down tight, sunglasses on, and the hood of my sweatshirt up each time I went in there, she might have taken me for a Unabomber copycat. After all, when the FBI arrested him fourteen years prior—almost to the day—it was at his cabin just seventy miles away, outside of Lincoln, Montana. On top of that, he was close to my age back then, and some people had told me in the past that I bear a striking resemblance to him.

I couldn't discern whether these thoughts had any credence or my paranoia was escalating to dangerous new heights. With my mind taking a shellacking from the whirlwind of frenetic events constantly spinning all around me for so long, my sense of judgment seemed dizzied at times. But half out of it or not, I did believe that Ted Kaczynski probably hadn't felt all that different about being hunted down than I did. Whether it was in my head or not, it just wasn't fair that I should even have to entertain such thoughts. I may have been a lot of things, but people like the Soleswatchers would have to look far and wide to find a more peace-loving person than myself.

Any way you slice it, the woman in the office did not like me. Maybe she abhorred everybody, but that was irrelevant. The bottom line was I had to pay up by eleven that morning or leave. And I just knew there would be a confrontation.

As I traipsed back to the camper, sipping my coffee from a foam cup, I heard a vehicle coming up the road behind me. Not bothering to turn around I just moved to the edge of the road and kept walking. The tires were crunching gravel very slowly, but when it caught up to me, I nearly jumped out of my Fruit of the Looms. I'd been so deep into my newest worry that by the time the big pickup truck approached I was barely aware of it. Stunning me back to the here and now when it appeared alongside me, the driver, only two feet away said, "Good morning stranger!"

Startled, I jerked my head around and my shoulders back. It was Julie Dubois.

"Hey…Julie…you caught me off guard. How are you?"

"I'm good, Tom. Can I give you a lift?"

"Ahhh, sure, my camper's just around that bend."

"I know, come on in."

She knew? How did she know that? What's she doing *here?* I asked myself.

I climbed up and into the silver behemoth, and she gave me a quick once-over saying, "Wow! Don't we look handsome? You shaved off your beard!"

Stroking my bare chin, as she started rolling ahead, I said, "Yeah, feels kind of naked, but I'm getting used to it."

"Well, you look terrific and a lot more rested than you did at my place."

Putting on a devilish smile now, I said, "Oh go on, I'll bet you tell all the boys that."

She, too, was still smiling. Keeping her eyes on the road, she leaned across the expansive front seat and gave me a playful shoulder slap. It was plain to see that she was genuinely happy to have found me. As for me, I was flattered that she had bothered to look in the first place. With her hair all tucked up and back, exposing her delicate ears and jaw line, she didn't look more beautiful than I'd remembered, that would be impossible, but she did look a snippet more glamorous.

A few moments later we got out of the truck, alongside the camper; and Solace was expressing all her usual excitement inside. Scrunching up my face a little, I tilted my head to one side, and looked at Julie out of the corner of my eyes. Teasingly, as if it was a mild scolding I said, "And just how did *you* know where my RV was?"

I could not believe it, but she was actually blushing like a schoolgirl. She lowered her pretty face and looked up at me, as if her pants had fallen down and she'd quickly hiked them up. "Well...I just happened to be in the neighborhood and..."

"Come on now. I was born at night, but not last night."

"Okay, today's Wednesday, I had to come into Missoula anyway. I have three classes at the university and just happened to wake up a little early. Sooo, I thought maybe I'd see if I could find you. See how you're doing."

Losing the face scrunch now, I said in a more serious tone, "Thank you Julie. That was very considerate. Hey, what do you say, want to meet Solace? Come on, let's get inside before she tears this thing apart."

Once Solace calmed down, she and Julie hit it off really well. Knowing what an excellent judge of character Solace is, I wouldn't have expected it to have worked out any other way. But still, I was quite surprised when she perched on Julie's lap after we sat on the sofa. Still with my own coffee, I asked her if she cared for any.

"No thanks, I'm pretty well coffee'd out. I don't have but about ten minutes anyway." Glancing around she then said, "Nice setup you have here, Tom. And I must say, very tidy, too. "

Since I was working on my first coffee of the morning, I reflexively picked up the pack of cigarettes laying on the end table. Then I put it right back down.

"No, go right ahead Tom. I don't mind if you smoke."

"Are you sure? I know some people are a little skittish about the secondhand smoke thing."

"No, go right ahead," she said waving me off. "I myself have a couple every afternoon, along with my two glasses of red wine. Sure, smoking, even in moderation, isn't going to improve anybody's health, but I sure as heck don't buy into all those ridiculous, government-bought, doomsday studies."

"I'm with you on that," I said, after lighting one up, "can you imagine the Surgeon General stating that, one inhale of secondhand smoke can sicken a nonsmoker for the rest of their life? They better stay out of New York then. Just walking the streets there, a person inhales the equivalent of a pack a day. Anyway, I'm glad you stopped over, Julie."

"Don't be silly. I really wanted to see if you were doing alright."

"Yeah, I'm doing considerably better than I was three days ago. Don't forget, the night I met you I'd just finished two days on the road. On top of that, I'd been going through an awful lot mentally. Julie," I said, feeling my eyes narrow, "have you ever heard of a website called Soleswatch.com?"

"That's part of the reason I came to see you today."

"What do you mean?"

"After you left my place Sunday, I got on the computer and did a little research. I'd been seeing you on the news all along, but after meeting you, I wanted to just browse a bit, and yes, I did see that mean-spirited Soleswatch nonsense. I saw that tracking page, too, and it got me thinking." Julie paused for a second or two then, while smoothing her hand over Solace's tawny head. I knew she was looking for just the right words.

"Tom...I didn't want to come looking for you right away. I knew you wanted to be, needed to be, *alone*."

"That was very thoughtful."

"Anyhow, I was thinking, since you'd last been spotted by those idiots in Wyoming, you'd be reasonably safe here in Montana, if you had a place where...oh hell, what I'm trying to say is, why don't you bring the camper back to my place?"

"I can't do that. I would never want to chance dragging you into my mess. And not only that, I'm just not..."

"I swear to you, Tom," she interrupted, "you can have your space, and I'll have mine. You can park anywhere you like on the property, and we can run a water hose to the RV. I also have a generator. Winter's all but over now, I won't be needing it. You can hook it up and have all the electric you need. I swear, it will almost be like you're out there alone. Come on, you don't need to be around people right now."

"I'm sorry, Julie, I just can't. Please understand."

"Tom, there's nothing to worry about. You can do your thing, I'll do mine. You'll hardly see me most days. I..."

"There are other reasons." I said, cutting her off, "It's not just about you being a woman and me being a man. Look, you have no idea how flattered I am that you've been so kind and taken such an interest in my welfare. It's just that...I can't"

Her chest expanded beneath her pink turtleneck sweater, as she drew in a long breath. She leaned her head back, looked up at the low ceiling, exhaled; then looked back at me.

"Okay, Tom. I thought it was a good idea, but I can't force you into something you don't want to do," she said as she reached into her purse. "But let me just give you my phone number, in case you have a change of heart."

As she rummaged through her purse, I said nothing. So badly, I wanted to go to her place but there was Elaina to think about. The temptation of being with this woman--this kind, generous, drop-dead-gorgeous woman--would be too great if I stayed there for any period of time. But I also felt like I was spitting on her benevolent offer. As if rejecting it was a tremendous display of disrespect and thanklessness. I thought how Elaina would never want me to stay so close to another woman so soon.

But then, something suddenly came to me from outside the box of my mind. It somehow just appeared in my consciousness, as if it had been sent there by Elaina. It told me, against all my previous beliefs, that Elaina would actually *want* me to go to Julie's. That she'd want more than anything that I be safe. And I believed it. This, I suddenly knew, was not rationalizing.

"Tom, are you alright?" Julie asked as she held out the small sheet of paper.

"Yeah, sure, I'm sorry! My mind was drifting off for a second. Listen Julie, you know what, I think I *will* take you up on your offer."

She looked at me as if she'd been shocked, and just as quickly, her face lit up, as if I'd just given her something she desperately needed. Like a kid who'd just laid eyes on a Christmas Morning bicycle.

"Really? That would be great! I promise you..."

133

"You don't have to promise me anything, Julie," I said, waving her off, "You're doing me a favor, a big favor. I really appreciate it. But there's just one thing we have to agree on."

"Go ahead. I'm listening."

"If anything happens that makes me think your safety is in jeopardy, I'm going to leave. Even if you think my reason is farfetched or totally crazy, you won't try to stop me. Is that a deal?"

"Fair enough."

Chapter 18

Entering Julie's clearing from the dirt road, the mountains were on the left; the river a few hundred yards to the right; and her cabin was straight ahead. I backed the camper--and its only license plate--close to the river, with the driver's side flush to a pine forest. It looked like a peaceful, cozy spot. Solace and I would be only steps from the river, and we'd enjoy that marvelous mountain view every time we looked through the wide windshield or sat outside.

It was too far from the cabin to run water hoses, but that was okay. The camper had a huge freshwater tank. It held enough to last me a few days at a time, so all I'd have to do when running low was drive to the spigot alongside Julie's cabin and fill it up. As for emptying the sewage, that was a simple matter also. Just as I had at Franklin Dewitt's place in Florida, I'd drive once a week to a dump station. The only difference was now, with that campground I'd stayed at being the only one yet open, I'd empty the tank at a truck stop instead. My biggest problem would be just across the field, inside that A-frame cabin.

Other than the early morning deer along the river bank and the occasional nighttime yips and howls of coyotes, the first two weeks of my stay were uneventful. And in a way, that bothered me. I'd only spoken to Julie one time. When she returned from her classes in Missoula that first day, she drove right over and checked to see if I needed anything. After we'd gone to her storage shed and brought back the generator, that was it. Being the days were still quite cool, neither of us spent much time outside. The two or three times we did see each other, all we did was exchange distant waves. She kept to herself, and I read a lot and tinkered around with the laptop. The only time I ventured outside the camper was to walk Solace or jog up and down the dirt road. And if at all possible, I tried to do that early in the morning or when the silver pickup truck was gone.

On two occasions, both around dusk, a sheriff's cruiser parked in front of Julie's cabin. Though it made me uneasy, I figured it must have been that fellow, Sean Garrity, she'd mentioned the night we'd met. Both times he only stayed about fifteen minutes. Both times I felt like a spy, as I kept peeking out the window. And yes, I suppose I was spying. But there was more to it than just being nosy. Each time I lifted the curtain I actually felt twinges of jealousy. Each time, I wondered what might be going on inside the cabin. Each time, I wished a little harder that I'd see the guy leave. Each time, I became a lot more disgusted with myself.

But that wasn't the only reason for my self-abhorrence. I also felt like a shit for being unsociable with Julie those first two weeks. She was going out on a limb for me; taking a chance that could have some very serious ramifications. And how was I showing my gratitude--by treating her like a leper. That's not to say my ignoring her didn't bother me. It bothered me deeply. Every night, after kissing Elaina's burgundy cap, I paid my penance. I tossed and flipped in that bed, as if it was a guilt-infested pit--a deep, murky pit with two beautiful faces watching my every move.

Although I felt the gesture would seem like an obvious admission of guilt; and in part was, I wanted to touch base with Julie. I had to talk to her, not that a gun was being held to my head, but I wanted to. For two days I kept looking out the windows but didn't see her once. The third afternoon was unseasonably warm, so I took Solace and two lawn chairs outside, along with hopes that Julie might come out. For the first time since I'd been out West, the temperature hit sixty degrees. Old Man Winter had finally loosened his frigid grip. Not a single cloud marred that part of "Big Sky Country" as I sat alongside the camper. By now the river was flowing faster than it had, and the sound of its water rushing over the rocks on such a gorgeous day was a soothing treat. To my left, The Bitterroots also seemed to have taken on a new life with the arrival of the first warm front.

After I soaked up the sun and took in all the beauty for half an hour, Julie's door opened. From a hundred yards across the grassy field, she waved again. This time I stood up, waved back and started toward her. As I quick-stepped closer, she waited, and I felt like a total ingrate. I felt like I was wearing a sandwich sign over my shoulders, and the nearer I got to her, the bigger the letters read, "Here comes the user, get ready for the lame excuses!" That's exactly how I felt after acting the way I had. Whether my reasons where viable or not, didn't seem to matter. I felt like a counterfeit, and my words seemed smarmy when I got close enough to say, "Julie, how are you?"

"Good, good...how are you liking this weather?" There was no resentment in her tone. I was surprised, and angry at myself for being surprised.

"It's gorgeous. So is your place. Sitting over there, I was just thinking it's like being in a national park."

"Well, it is in a way, we are surrounded by a national forest," she said, kneeling down, giving Solace a brisk two-handed rub. Then, looking back up at me with as much concern in her words as her face, she asked, "So...how are you adapting, Tom?"

"Pretty well. Other than a little cabin fever, I'm okay, I guess."

"Hey," she said, straightening up with a smile, "how about a beer? I'm ready for my afternoon wine. We can sit in back. I have a small deck."

"Sure, I'd like that."

"Great! Meet you in back."

I walked around the cabin while she went in for the drinks. For the first time, Solace had a close view of the two horses, back just a ways, standing in front of the stable. I had her on the leash, of course, but was amazed when she didn't make a peep. Maybe she figured if they were okay with Julie, they were okay with her.

I felt very safe there, safe as I could possibly be. I took a seat on a wooden bench and studied the tree line beyond the grassy back field.

"I hope you don't mind Coors beer," Julie said, as she came out the back, using her elbow to prevent the screen door from slamming.

My Lord, she looked gorgeous again, her hair brushed down so nicely; beige jeans this time, black boots, and yet another cowboy shirt. This one black with white piping across the chest, and it fit just as snug as the others I'd seen. I, like most men, take great pleasure seeing an attractive woman over and over in different outfits. Each time it's like seeing a different version of her, each time it's a special treat.

"Coors is fine, Julie, thanks," I said, taking the bottle.

"What have you been up to?" she asked, sitting in a chair next to the bench.

"Just kind of laying low, jogging in the mornings, reading, fooling around with a journal I've been keeping."

"A journal," she said, as if it was a question.

"Yes, something I've been tinkering with since I...since *we* left New York."

"Hmmm," she said, sipping from her wineglass, looking over its rim at me. "Is it something you might want to publish?"

"I'm toying with the idea. Of course, I'm not finished living it out yet, and I don't even know that I ever will live it out to the end."

After she lit the first of her ritualistic afternoon cigarettes and exhaled, she asked in a very sympathetic tone, "Has it been that hard, Tom? Or maybe I shouldn't be asking about..."

"No, no, it's okay. Let me ask you, Julie, did you ever read or hear about what happened at our apartment when Elaina and I returned from Stockholm?"

"Yes. It was all over the news."

I gave her a small smile, but it wasn't easy. It was to let her know I really hadn't minded her asking. Then I said, "I've been keeping everything that happened since that day inside, everything...everything except what I told the authorities in North Carolina about what happened to Elaina." I choked up then. My voice broke slightly, and tears welled in the corners of my eyes. I wiped them with the sleeve of my sweatshirt.

"I'm sorry, Julie, excuse me."

Now looking like she was about to cry, she stood up, sat alongside me on the bench, and put her hand on my quivering shoulder.

"It's okay Tom. You'll be alright. I can only imagine what you've been through."

"I'm sorry," I said, sniffling and dragging my fingertips across both my eyes. "It's all been so very difficult. I haven't had anybody to talk to about it. My mind has constantly felt like it's being squeezed, from every direction…by an enormous pressure."

"That's too much for anyone to take," she assured me, as she gently massaged my shoulder.

Looking at her now, I felt as if I'd known Julie for a long, long time. I didn't know if we would ever share any kind of a future together. I didn't know if I'd ever allow it, or if she would even want it. But it certainly did feel like we had a past; a warm, comforting, close past. It was almost as if we'd been married once, in a previous life, in a faraway place. Maybe my senses had gone completely haywire, I don't know, but the feeling was there, and it was as profound as it was undeniable.

As if confessing to someone I knew well and loved deeply, I said, "Are you sure you want to hear all this, Julie?"

"You bet I do."

That afternoon, under the warm Montana sun, in one of the most beautiful places I'd ever seen, I told Julie Dubois most everything that had happened. From the kittens in the apartment to my last confrontation with that woman in the Colorado campground, I hardly left out a thing. I told her about the *Enough is Enough* bumper stickers and all the livid Soles haters I'd run into. I told her about Arturo Giovanni, and that I'd called him, and his estranged wife had answered and told me he had passed on. I told her my book had been dropped, and that Denise Solchow, my editor, had been fired, as she'd suspected. I told her Denise had hooked up with another publisher, a smaller one, and that they were going to pick up *Enough is Enough*. I told her Manny Ruiz, back in New York, had cleaned out my apartment for me and stored the few things I asked him to. When I finally told her how I came up with Solace's name, I could tell she'd already figured that out. It felt so easy and natural talking to her that I even went into detail about what took place on that North Carolina nature trail.

When I finally finished and she'd gotten us both a fresh drink, she sat back down and said, "I don't know how anybody could go through all that and keep their sanity, Tom."

"Well…I don't know how much of my sanity is left or how long it will last, but I'm doing the best I can."

"You'll be alright in the end. It's easy to see you're a very strong man."

"Maybe I am, maybe I'm not, but with no end to all this in sight, I really don't know how long I can hold out."

One of the few things I hadn't told her was about the Glock and what I almost did with it at that Florida rest stop three months earlier. Wanting to bump the conversation in a less somber direction now, I said, "How about you, Julie? You've got one heck of a nice place here. This scenery has to be some of God's finest work, but what brought you all the way out here…to Montana, from New Hampshire?"

Turning her head to the side for a moment, she looked into the towering mountains alongside us. It was if she was searching for something in them. The expression on her face went from sympathetic to nostalgic. Then she looked back at me and said, "It's more a question of what *pushed me out* of New Hampshire."

I took a sip of beer, then said, "Maybe it's something *you* don't want to talk about. If not, I understand."

"I was married once also, Tom."

"I kind of figured that. You're a very attractive lady."

Waving me off, she allowed herself a brief smile. But it melted as quickly as it arrived, and she said, "Sixteen years…I was very happy for sixteen years. Then, in the end, the last two years, well, I never in my life saw anybody change like he did."

"Was it another woman?"

"No, if there was another woman, I didn't know about her. It was two other things. First, he started gambling. Up until our fourteenth anniversary, he'd never in his life gone to a casino, a racetrack or anyplace like that. Neither had I, but I thought it would be fun. But then I…I guess I blew it."

"*You* blew it? How do you figure? He was the one with the problem, right?"

"Yes, but I started it all. It was my idea. You see, on our fourteenth, I asked him if he wanted to take a ride down to Connecticut, go to one of the casinos. I figured since it was almost three hours away from where we lived in Portsmouth, we'd spend the night in a motel, have a little getaway. Heck, he didn't even want to go. He was probably the only man in America to do a stint in the military and never once play cards. He didn't even know how to play poker."

"Okayy, but what did you do wrong?"

Julie then paused and lit her second cigarette. She exhaled toward the sky and continued, "I asked him a second time, and he said yes. I know he only agreed because it was our anniversary. He'd always been somewhat considerate. Anyway, we drove down there and the worst possible thing happened."

"What was that?"

"We won. He won. For a few hours we'd win and lose, a little here and there, but slowly the machines whittled away the hundred and fifty dollars we each came with. I lost all mine, and he only had about thirty dollars left, no, I remember, it was exactly thirty-two. Anyway, I looked at my watch and it was way past dinner time. The time had flown by, and we were both starved. I suggested we give it up and get something to eat. He agreed but wanted to put the last of his money into a five dollar machine. He figured he'd lose it in six pulls and we'd leave. Up to that point, we'd only been playing a dollar a spin.

Anyway, he gets nothing on the first spin, but on the second he wins twenty-three hundred dollars."

"That must have been exciting."

"Yes it was, and it didn't end there. He still had twenty dollars from his original one-fifty, so that left four more spins. After that we were going to take the money and run. But no, on his very last spin he won another nineteen-hundred. We walked out of there with forty-two hundred dollars."

"That's a lot of money. You both must have felt pretty good after that, but I think I know where this is going."

"We had no problems financially, Tom. I did okay teaching at the community college, and he did so-so selling furniture, but it wasn't cheap living in Portsmouth. Even though we had a modest house, the mortgage payments and taxes were quite high. So was everything else, you know, heating bills and all that.

At any rate, being it was wintertime and there wasn't all that much to do, two weeks after winning we decided to go back to that casino. This time we lost three-hundred each, and he insisted we take another six from an ATM. Needless to say, we lost. I was cured. I had no desire to go back after that, but he sure did. Since he worked in retail and had mostly weekdays off, he started going to Connecticut while I was teaching. In a year and a half, he went through forty-seven-thousand dollars. Almost everything we'd saved. "

"Geez, that's a crime. I'm sure you tried to stop him. You had to know what was going on."

"Of course, and we started to fight. I begged and pleaded with him to stop at first, but it soon escalated into all-out fights. He started drinking a lot, especially when he couldn't go gambling. Then things got real ugly, real fast."

"That gambling can become a real horror," I said. "If someone has an addictive personality, they can easily get hooked on it. I know people back in New York who became consumed by it. One couple lost their dry-cleaning business, and shortly after that, their marriage went all to hell. No, let me correct that, I know two couples who lost all their money and wound up getting divorced."

"It gets worse, Tom. You see, when he was drinking he started getting a little quick with his hands. And he was a big guy, six-five."

"You mean he hit you?"

"At first it started with just shoving. *Just shoving...*would you listen to me? Anyway, after a while, he started coming home from the Connecticut casinos not only broke but drunk as well. It was a miracle he never got caught--driving a hundred and fifty miles in the condition he was in. But he did drive and he did get plenty drunk, and when he'd get home, all hell would break loose. I'd give him all sorts of hell, and he'd get belligerent and right in my face. I got tired of that fast. One night, after it had happened a few times, I put my hands on his chest and told him to get away."

Julie paused then and shook her head. For a moment she was back in time. I could tell because the hurt was visible all over her delicate face. She managed to keep the corners of her mouth from drooping, but it was easy to see the pain hadn't completely left her yet. When you are stabbed by the knife of a loved one, their blade is always the sharpest and the wound the deepest.

Her brown eyes were now moist, and that deep hurt reflected clearly in them as she went on, "I only put my hands on his chest, Tom. I didn't push him. I just laid them there. In a way, they were begging, pleading with him to be the man he had always been. For a long time, he was a thoughtful, good man, and we were very close. Our minds had always been attuned to each other's. All I wanted was for the gambling and drinking to stop. He was going through our life savings, drifting away from me, and ruining our marriage."

"I never could comprehend how a man could hit a woman," I said, as I straightened up on the bench, still looking at Julie alongside me, "especially a good man. I don't know, I suppose some people, even the ones you'd never suspect, can have a bit of the beast lurking inside them."

"I suppose," she said, looking more angry than hurt now. "But his beast broke out the first time he shoved me. We were in our kitchen, my palms on his chest like I said, and he pushed me so hard I flew back and hurt my back on the table. When I hit it, my legs came to a stop, but my back flexed so far back I could barely get out of bed for four days. He pushed me, I don't know, two or three times after that, and he was always sorry in the morning. But it wasn't good enough. The irreparable damage had already been done. Then, the last time we went face to face, with my fifteen-year-old daughter standing right there, screaming for us to stop, he slammed me in the side of my face with the heel of his hand. It was just like a punch, Tom, and he knocked me out cold. When I came to he was gone. I called the police, and that was the end. I pressed charges, and he was put away for five years."

"I don't know what to say, Julie. I am so sorry. I just don't understand how..."

"That's okay," she interrupted, slowly waving her hand to one side, "I'm long over him now. It's just that an experience like that, with someone you were so sure you knew, makes it awfully hard to totally trust anyone ever again. I was never what you'd call a gullible person. I've always considered myself a pretty good judge of character, but when something like that happens, with somebody you were so close to...well, it pretty much shoots all to hell your faith in people. Can you blame me?"

Of course, I told her I didn't blame her. After she got us another two drinks, we talked some more. We were getting deeper and deeper into each other's souls. She told me her daughter, Marcy, was her only child. That they'd moved to Montana six years earlier. Julie's mother had died when she was in her twenties, and her father passed on shortly after her marriage went all to hell. He'd owned two hardware stores in the Portsmouth area and when he died, Julie and her two sisters sold them and split the proceeds. That's where she'd gotten the money to buy her Montana place. Once Marcy graduated high school, being young and bored to tears in the country, she went back to New Hampshire. She'd been accepted at Keene State College, and was, by this time, finishing her senior year.

I really enjoyed myself that afternoon. Our conversation had been, by far, the longest I'd had with anyone since Elaina's death. Even during the two months I'd stayed at Franklin Dewitt's in Florida, we never spent more than an hour or so conversing. Though Franklin turned out to be a genuine prince, our talks were mostly about guy stuff. With Julie it had been much deeper, and I was finally able to tell somebody about what I'd been through. Not only that, but I was getting very close to this woman and she seemed to feel the same way about me. But when the sun was just about to set behind the mountains, it got cold, and it was time to leave. Though I was curious (so to speak) and thought about it more than once, I hadn't asked Julie about Sean Garrity's visits. There were two reasons for this. Number one, who she saw was certainly none

144

of my business; and number two, I knew I had to keep myself from getting too close to Julie Dubois.

But that wall of discipline I was trying to keep intact could not keep out all my emotions. As I walked back to the camper with Solace in the fading daylight, I suddenly felt a stab of jealousy--a sharp, piercing stab. Sean Garrity had entered the clearing from the entry road in his sheriff's cruiser. He was a good distance away, but I could still see his face beneath the low-tilted brim of his cowboy hat. He saw me, too. I lifted my hand the casual way men do when they say hello. He didn't react right away. He kept his eyes on me for a moment, as he continued toward Julie's. Eventually, he gave me a slow nod. It was really a slow half-nod, and there was nothing friendly about it.

Chapter 19

Over the next month and a half, I didn't once make eye contact with Garrity again. For one reason or another, he was showing up at Julie's place far less often. But she and I sure saw quite a bit of each other. She took me horseback riding a few times, which was a first for me. For two full days, I helped her repair the split rail fence around her small corral. She cooked dinner for me several times and since the spring weather was rapidly improving, we spent more and more time together on her back deck.

In the beginning, we talked often about my plans to go to Maine and what I'd do after getting there. Every time one of us brought it up, Julie acted a little sadder, and I'd get a hollow feeling inside that seemed to be swelling. After a while, I made a concentrated effort not to bring the subject up, and if she happened to, I immediately swayed the conversation in a different direction. We were becoming very, very close. The distance I tried to keep between us was constantly shrinking. What was not shrinking was our cerebral and physical attraction to each other. That was undeniable. The more we got together, the harder it got for me to keep Elaina between us. But I was vigilant and would not give in. Then, one evening after that sixth week of my stay, another force came between us.

I was sitting outside the camper with Solace, taking in another peaceful sunset when Sean Garrity rolled into the clearing again. This time he didn't go to the cabin. He made a right turn and drove across the new grass towards me. I still hadn't met him and hadn't allowed myself to ask Julie about him.

When the cruiser got close, I stood up and tried to quiet Solace down. She wouldn't stop. Her barking was fiercer than usual and mixed with growls. I opened the camper door and lifted her inside.

"Hi there," I said a moment later, ducking down to the passenger window, looking at Garrity on the other side of a computer and an upright rifle.

No answer. Instead he opened his door, stood up, and walked around the front of the car towards me. I just stood there watching. If it wasn't for his hat, he'd have been about the same height as me. He looked a wee bit bulkier and maybe ten years younger; right about Julie's age. His sideburns were gray, trimmed close, and he carried himself like a brigadier general.

"Sooo, "he said, standing in front of me, first assessing the camper then sizing me up, "Julie tells me you're her cousin from back east."

I had no idea she'd told him that and tried to hide my surprise. Glancing at his wry smile then back at his narrowed eyes, I said, "You're Sean, right?"

"Yupper, I'm Sean alright."

"Well, I'm pleased to meet..." I started to say, extending my hand.

But he wouldn't have any part of it. He put his hands on his hips instead, just above his gun belt, and interrupted, "Look, *friend*, let's not beat around the bush here. I know you're not her cousin."

"Whoooa, hold on, I never said I was," I came back as I dropped my hand. "And what does it matter? I'm a friend of Julie's."

"You're more than that. I know exactly who you are. You're that Soles character." His eyes narrowed even more now, like two spiteful slits, and his jaw muscles undulated as he ground his molars.

Already, I'd had about as much of this nasty-spirited harassment as I was going to take.

"You know something; I don't like being called a character. And yes, I am Thomas Soles, but I haven't broken any laws. I don't have time for this, and I don't like your attitude. Now, why don't you get to the point? What exactly do you want?"

"I'll tell you what I want. Me and some other people 'round here want you out of these parts. You don't like the way this

147

country's being run, you don't like the job people are doing, the job I'm doing. I want you out of here."

I wasn't ready for this and didn't need to hear it. After actually relaxing at Julie's for so long, not having a single confrontation with anyone, I was no longer used to this kind of treatment. And I wasn't going to put up with it.

"And what happens if I don't want to leave...my *friend?*"

"Oh, you'll leave one way or another."

"Are you threatening me?" I said, as hot-adrenaline rushed through my arms, and my hands tightened at my sides. I did not care anymore. After all I'd been through for six tortuous months, nothing mattered at this moment. As if I'd returned to the streets of my youth, with that newspaper still stuffed in my shoes and mayonnaise sandwiches in my belly, I said, "Because, if you *are* threatening me, maybe we can settle it right here and now."

He took a step closer, so close that the brim of his hat almost touched my forehead. Solace was going absolutely insane at the window behind me. Garrity now dropped his hands to his sides as if at the ready. Jutting his jaw at me he said, "You threatening a law officer?"

"You're not on the clock are you? You have a problem, maybe we can work it out. I'm not going to just stand here and take your shit."

Then there was a loud shriek. "HEY STOP! WHAT THE HELL IS GOING ON OVER THERE!" It was Julie. She was running across the grass towards us.

"Just remember Soles, I want you out of here. I'll give you two days."

I just glared at him.

"Remember," he said, "two days."

Then, just as Julie came up to us, he took a step back and slowly turned around.

"What's going on here," she demanded, as she got right up in his face, looking at him with so much fire in her eyes it could have scorched him.

With a calm tone and a forced smile he said, "It's okay, Julie, I was just introducing myself to your cousin here."

148

She glanced at me, got nothing out of my eyes, then glared back at him.

"I think you better leave, Sean. I'm not real happy right now. It isn't a good time for a visit."

"Sure, no problem, if that's the way you feel about it. It's just about time to start my patrol anyway."

Then he looked back at me and said, "Don't forget now, be sure to get another license plate for the front of your RV. I'd hate to see you get ticketed for that. You could run into another law officer who isn't quite as friendly as me."

Then something dawned on me. I thought, *How does he know I have a New York Plate on the back bumper? I'm backed right up to the river. Ohhh...that-son-of-a-bitch! Unless he'd seen me driving to the truck stop to empty sewage one of those times, he's been surveilling me from the far bank—spying on me. That's it! I know that's what he's been doing.*

"Yeah, you bet. I'll order another plate right away." I said as he skirted the front of his car.

Julie and I watched as Garrity drove away. When he was out of sight, she said, "What happened, Tom? What was all that about?"

I could see the disappointment in her face and hear it in her voice. She sounded like a little girl who'd been having a terrific time at her birthday party, only to have it ruined. Although I'd been cautious all along, and she'd picked up on it, I know she'd been enjoying my company and wouldn't want anything to jeopardize it.

"I'm sorry this had to happen, Julie. I knew eventually something like this would happen. Look...it's getting chilly out here, why don't we go inside."

We climbed into the camper, and Solace stopped barking as if on cue. As soon as Julie sat on the sofa, she was all over her, licking her face and doing the high-speed pendulum thing with her tail. Julie was a sport about it, and she even managed to smile. But it didn't last. After a moment or two, I told Solace to get down.

Sitting opposite Julie in a swivel rocker by now, speaking with my eyes, as well as my lips, I said, "We both knew this day would come, didn't we? We didn't know who or what would upset everything, but we knew something would."

"Dammit, Tom, what in the hell happened out there?"

"Oh, what's the sense of going into it? The bottom line is your friend knows who I am. He told me you said I was your cousin, but obviously he's run my license plates at the sheriff's department. Look...I don't know what kind of relationship you have with him, that's none of my business, but he, and what he calls *other* people, don't want me around here."

"I don't have what I'd call a relationship with him, Tom. I dated him twice, when I first moved here. That was it. Once or twice a week, before he goes to work, he stops over to make sure I'm okay back here. Sometimes he has a quick cup of coffee."

"It seems to me he's looking for more than coffee."

"I realize that. It's obvious. I've given him enough hints that I'm not interested. All this time I never wanted to be rude. I considered him a friend, but that's over now. Next time I see him I'm going to let him know he's not, in no uncertain terms."

Holding up my palm, rotating my head slowly, I said, "No, Julie, don't do that. The last thing I want is to be responsible for you losing a friend. Had I never come here, nothing would have changed for you."

"I'm sorry, but I don't care what you say. I'm going to tell him and tell him good."

"Look Julie," I said, leaning forward in the chair, my elbows on my knees, "I told you...one thing like this happens, and I'm gone."

"I don't care what happened, Tom. I want you to stay. Do you understand what I'm telling you here?" She had that ruined-party look again, but this time there were tears forming in the corners of her straining dark eyes. I got up and sat next to her on the sofa.

"Julie, don't. Please!"

It cut at me to see her like this. I put my arm around her shoulder, felt it trembling.

"Don't. Come on. It's not the end of the world. We can keep in..."

"Can't you see," she interrupted, the tears now coursing her cheeks, "I love you, Tom! I don't want you to leave here." Then she threw her arms around my neck and buried her face in it.

I embraced her also, with both arms, and when I did, she began to cry--her hurt and disappointment burst from her eyes. With each profuse sob, her warm body quaked against mine. Every shudder was another reminder of just how precious she was. Just how lucky I was to have someone so special care about me so much. Forget the human contact aspect that I hadn't felt for so many months and so desperately needed, this woman in my arms meant far more than that. Though it was the first time I'd felt her body tight against mine, it felt ever so natural, as if we'd done it a thousand times before. I knew we were both exactly where we belonged. We now shared the same soul--very much like I had with my Elaina for so many years. But there were differences. This time there were obstructions. This time there were hurdles. And I knew I couldn't make it over them, not yet.

Julie slowly lifted her head from the crook of my neck. We were almost nose to nose now. Her cheeks were moist and her eyes slightly puffed. But the sadness in her face, edged by her long flowing hair, so black and so sleek, somehow made her more beautiful than ever. Looking into my eyes, no, beyond them, hoping to see the same feelings she had in her heart, she said, "I'm sorry, Tom. Don't get mad at me. But I can't hold this back, even if I should." She then leaned closer and gently laid her lips on mine.

Slowly, as if asking for permission, she offered her tongue. I accepted. Our mouths parted, and that most intense ancient ritual two people can share began. The meeting of our tongues was tentative at first, welcoming exploring, massaging, but the undeniable pull of desire soon aroused desperate, hot yearnings through both our minds and bodies. Soon our breathing became labored and rapid. It seemed the camper was quickly becoming a vacuum, with less and less oxygen remaining. Fragmented visions of Elaina kept snapping in and out of my mind--like mild, short-lived electrical shocks. With each jolt, I asked myself, six months, is that long enough?

Then I felt Julie's hand work its way between our chests. She began unbuttoning her blouse. I eased my lips from hers. Her hand froze and she opened her eyes. We looked at each other for a long moment. Trying to see beyond the passion and lust in my eyes, I said, "I'm still going to have to leave, Julie. I might be gone forever, I might not. I can't tell you for sure. Are you sure you want this?"

"Take me, Tom. I want you. I know I love you. I know *how much* I love you. After tonight is over, if all I'll have left is hope, I'll settle for that. I want you more than I've ever wanted anything."

Then she did it. She slid her hand down between us, between my legs, found what she was looking for and held me. "Take me, Tom. Take me now."

And I did. We went into the bedroom. I closed the door behind us. It was pretty dark by now, and I was glad. Whether I could have seen it or not from where I stood I don't know, but I refused to look in the direction of the nightstand. I could not look at Elaina's burgundy cap. I thought about whisking it onto the floor, but I didn't. Instead I made love to Julie Dubois. I fell in love with Julie Dubois. And just before we consummated that most profound expression of human love, amidst all its sensuality and fervor, I took one short moment to look at the woman beneath me and say, "I love you, Julie."

Chapter 20

After my jog early the next morning, while working on my second cup of coffee with the laptop on my knees, I posted the camper for sale on Craigslist. Knowing I'd be leaving Montana for Maine the next day, I wanted to make one quick effort to sell it. The odds weren't very good, but it was a Sunday, and most people would be off from work. I figured maybe something could happen. The idea of driving the Winnebago across two thirds of the country was unsettling to say the least. Plus, I knew I wouldn't need it once I reached my destination. The plan was to buy that small, isolated place somewhere in northern Maine. I knew from experience the few scattered villages in those North Woods were not only secluded and sparsely populated, but beautiful as well. There were some fine places where Solace and I had at least a chance of being left alone.

With Julie being off the next two days, we planned to spend as much time together as possible. Sunday morning Solace and I had breakfast at the cabin. In the afternoon, we went back over to relax out on the deck. We'd only been sitting on the wooden bench maybe ten, fifteen minutes when my cell phone chimed.

The caller was a man from Missoula. He wanted to come over with his family to take a look at the camper. I was hopeful he would, but as I spoke into the phone, it became quite obvious Julie wasn't at all happy. The glow on her face faded as she listened intently. Though we had talked the whole thing through after breakfast, she knew this very well could be another step closer to my leaving. Hearing my conversation made my imminent departure seem all the more a reality, and that much closer. As fine a spring day as it was, that phone call took all the joy out of the Montana Spring sunshine. Our moods deflated, as if we suddenly had to rush to a funeral neither of us wanted to attend. It felt like a slow procession as the three of us made our way across the grassy field to wait by the camper.

It wasn't an hour later that a rusted-out Dodge Caravan preceded a trail of rising dust as it entered the clearing. Before it turned right and headed our way, we could see there were several children in the back. Either the muffler was shot or there was a bad leak in the exhaust system because it sounded as bad as the rest of the van looked. As it slowed to a stop, we saw through the windshield a young man in the driver's seat and a woman about the same age alongside him. She was thin and visibly drawn, as was the man, beneath a red ball cap.

After he killed the engine it sputtered, choked, and wretched like a three-pack-a-day smoker, and Solace started doing what she does best. Always the good trooper, Julie volunteered to walk her until she calmed down. As she coaxed Solace with the leash, the man turned to the children in the back of the van and said something. Then only the parents climbed out. They were worn alright, but their clothes looked reasonably clean and their long hair was combed. Nevertheless, I thought for sure this showing was going to be all for naught. *Where*, I wondered, *are these people ever going to come up with fourteen-thousand?*

"Lo there," the man said, extending his hand. He couldn't have been more than twenty-five, but his boney hand was hard and his palms and fingers calloused--like they'd been working for two lifetimes. The jeans they both wore looked like they'd been around a long time, too, but as I said, they were clean. His accent came right out of the Deep South when he went on, "I'm Jerrod Lockerby, and this here's muh wife, Jennie."

Tom, Tom Soles," I said, nodding a greeting to him then his wife. "So...you folks are looking for an RV?" I said.

"Yeah, me Jennie 'n our three kids have been livin' outta' the van for most of ten months now, down in Luzianna. That's where we're from. I've been workin' two jobs and a savin' all that time so's we could move up here to Mon-tana. We managed to put together enough to get up here and try to get settled. Jus' got here yesterday."

I was curious to find out what kind of places they'd spent so many nights in but didn't want to sound like I was prying. Homelessness had become a rampant societal disease in this country. I knew that in places such as California this human tragedy was so bad, there were entire parking lots designated for people who lived in their vehicles. I'd heard that when the unfortunates were allowed in for the night, the lots quickly filled to capacity. I was sure the Lockerby's had slept in places far worse and that their story wasn't a pretty one. I asked Jerrod, "Where did you stay down there, RV parks, places like that?"

"We'd do that a couple of times a week, you know, so we and the kids could freshen up and such. But them places ain't too cheap anymore, and a lot of 'em wouldn't let us spend the night because this here ain't a camper," he said, swooping his hand back toward his van.

"I hear you there," I said nodding my head, "so you want to step up to a camper now."

"Yup, that's what we were hopin'," Jenny Lockerby said. Then raising her eyes to the camper, they suddenly came to life. Looking at it adoringly, she said, "Wow...this is some beauty! Can we have a looksee inside?"

"Well, of course, here, let me get the door for you."

As I held it and they climbed in, I glanced at the blonde-haired kids in the van. They looked to be from three to six years old, and each of them had hopeful looks on their faces. From behind the window, they all waved at me and wore smiles as wide as the country they'd just crossed. It was easy to see these were well-behaved children. Somehow, they also seemed happy. Surely, they'd been dreaming for a long time about having some sort of home. I waved and smiled back. Then I gave Julie, who'd been watching all along, a little finger wave and followed Jerrod and Jennie inside the camper.

They absolutely loved it. Jennie stroked the three-burner stove as if it was a thing of her dreams. They both figured--if Montana didn't work out for them, they could always start up the engine and try their luck somewhere else. At least they'd have a home. When Jennie asked if she could show the kids the inside, I said sure. Jerrod then asked if we could step outside and talk.

"Mister Soles," he said, after we'd walked around the outside, "I really want to buy yer camper. It's a real beauty, and my Jennie, well, you can tell she likes it, too. But I have one problem."

"What's the problem, Jerrod?"

"Well," he said lifting his red cap, stroking back his hair, "I don't want to sound like no finagler, 'cause I'm not. I'm just talkin' man to man is all, being honest."

"Go ahead," I said in an understanding tone, nodding my head, letting him know I'd consider whatever it was he had to say."

"Anyway..." he took a deep breath as he glanced to the grass at his feet, let it back out when he looked back at me, "all I got is fourteen-thousand-five-hunert dollars in the world, Mistuh Soles. I know I'm gonna need 'bout five hunert more n' that with the tax, plates, and all that. What I'm tryin' to say here is...and please, don't get mad or insulted or anything...what I'm tryin' to say is I could give you twelve thousand. That's the most I can. I gotta have the other twenty-five hunert for..."

"No, Jerrod," I interrupted, "I can't take your twelve..."

"That's okay," he cut in, struggling to put a smile on his tired, disappointed face, "I unnerstand. This here's a fine unit, and I know what you're askin' is more than fair."

He put out his hand to show there were no hard feelings, and I took it. As we shook, I said, "Congratulations, Jerrod, you just bought your family a new home."

"Whaddaya mean, Mistuh Soles? I thought you jus' said ya couldn't take twelve."

"Yes, I did say that, but I don't want twelve from you. I just want ten-thousand dollars, and I'm going to give you the keys and title. I want you and your family to have this camper, and I want you to have enough left over so you have a fair chance of making it up here."

"Hot damn, I, I don't know what to say," he said, wiping both his glazed eyes with the back of his hand. "You can't imagine how happy I am right now. You don't know how good Jennie and the kids are going feel."

This young man, who hadn't caught a break in a long time, was fighting hard not to cry. I knew the deepest source of his tears was the hardship he and his family had suffered, but there was tremendous relief in them as well.

I patted him on the back saying, "Why don't you dry your eyes, Jerrod. Then we can go inside and tell everyone the good news."

The following morning, shortly after the banks opened, the Lockerby's returned with a cashier's check. I didn't tell them, but right after my early jog I'd driven the camper to the truck stop and filled it with gas. Of course, I had told Julie the afternoon before what the young family had endured for so long and about the deal I had given Jerrod.

As they drove the camper out of the clearing, Julie and I watched with heartfelt smiles until Jerrod, followed by Jennie in the dilapidated van, turned onto the dirt road and disappeared into the trees. But our contentment did not last. The moment they were out of sight that peaceful, benevolent feeling Julie and I had shared left with them. The next order of business was to go into Missoula and shop for a car for me.

Julie and I brought my few belongings to her place. She put the cats in the back bedroom, and we left Solace with the run of the cabin. She didn't like being left behind, but with the inevitable test-drives and negotiation process in front of us, there was no way we could bring her along.

We checked out a considerable number of dealerships and used car lots before I zeroed in on something I liked; a maroon, six-year-old Subaru Outback. I'd been adamant about buying a four-wheel drive for the Maine winters and despite this one's age, it only had 31,000 miles on the odometer. It also had very dark, tinted windows which was a big plus. Other than a little superficial rust on the undercarriage, the car was in fine shape. It was obvious it had been loved by its previous owners, just as the camper had been before I bought it back in New Jersey.

With Julie by my side in the showroom and all the salesmen, young and old, ogling at her, I played the necessary games for an hour and a half before closing the deal. By the time I jumped through the last hoop and was handed the keys and temporary plates, it was four in the afternoon. When I finally followed Julie's pickup out of the lot, it felt like I had put in a full day's work. But it had been worth it. Not only was I confident I'd bought a dependable vehicle for a relatively fair price, but I also felt much safer. It was far less conspicuous than the camper. No longer did the legions of Soles Haters know what I'd be driving, unless there had been a devout member at the dealership who recognized me. If there hadn't been, all I had to do next was pick up Solace and my things at Julie's--without Sean Garrity seeing me. If I could pull that off, I just might remain anonymous on the long trip back east.

As I tailed Julie on the Interstate, the Bitterroots before us grew larger with every mile marker we passed. Swelling even more than the mountains was the mixture of anxiety and dread I felt. I was very concerned Garrity might see me. As for the dread, there were two parts to that spirit-sapping emotion. Not only did I have to say goodbye to a woman I had come to love, but I had to do it quickly. And that certainly isn't the kind of thing anybody should have to rush through.

For me to have found someone like Julie Dubois in this day and age was like finding the way from chaos to nirvana. As I steered the Subaru behind her silver pickup, I damn well realized how fortunate I was to have a person like her care so much for me. I wanted more than anything to stay with her, start a new life. I was sure of that. But three obstacles were standing in my way, and I wasn't sure I'd ever get over or around them. And that's exactly what I told Julie an hour later when I was ready to leave her place.

With the sun setting behind those beautiful mountains and the Subaru all loaded up, I took a nervous glance at the entry road as I opened the passenger door for Solace. After she hopped in, I closed the door and turned to Julie for possibly the last time ever. Looking up at me, her eyes squinting from the pain she was trying to fight off, she tried to be strong. She took my hand in both of hers and said, "Tom, we can work everything out. We belong together. And I'm willing to do whatever I have to."

"Julie, I can't stay, not now. Maybe down the road we'll be able to work something out." I dropped my head, massaged my temples then looked back at her. "Look, you know I care for you deeply...you know I love you, but I've got those things I told you about working against me."

"Yeah, I know," she said, as her eyes began to well up, "but I don't give a good goddamn about taking chances. I just told you I'm willing to do anything to be with you."

"I'm sorry," I said softly, "I am not going to jeopardize your life. I checked that fucking Soleswatch last night. They know I'm here now."

"That son-of-a-bitch, Sean! They've really tracked you to Missoula? He better never show his face…"

"No, Julie. I don't want you complicating your life for me. Just let it go. Act like you don't know about it. Go back to the life you led before I came along."

With that, she dropped my hand and put hers on her waist. Jutting her face closer to mine she said, "Are you out of your mind, Tom? My life is never going to be the same again. Damn it", she went on, now with tears in her lashes, "you're part of me now. You're inside my heart, Tom. I can't shove anything I want in or out of there. You're there and you're going to stay there."

Putting my hands on her small shoulders, kneading them gently, I shot another quick look at the road again then said, "If I could spend whatever time I have left with you, Julie, and I knew nothing would happen to you, I would stay. I, I would kill myself if what happened to…to Elaina happened to you too. I refuse to…"

"Hold it, Tom. I know Elaina is still between us, and if you stayed she'd always be there. I would never expect you to just forget her. That's impossible. She's been part of you for far too long. I also know that you feel guilty about what you and I shared the other night. But I know this, too…I am dead sure that if you stayed with me, together, as time passed, I'd become a part of you, too."

"You already are! You know that, Julie."

Then I took one last nervous glance at the road and said, "I've got to go. Sean could be pulling into here any second now. I don't want to complicate this mess anymore than…"

"This mess, is that what you think this is?" Julie asked, breaking down into tears now.

I threw my arms around her and held her as tightly as I dared.

"Stop talking that nonsense," I said, rocking her slowly, "I need time, Julie. I've got to see if I can pull myself together. Maybe someday we'll figure out a way to work all this out. I promise; I'll try my hardest to think of something. But listen to me," I said, leaning my head back now, looking into her eyes again, "there's no time now. I've got to get out of here."

We kissed then. It was a long, lovely, heartfelt declaration of love that neither of us ever wanted to end. When I finally pulled my lips from hers, she said, "I'll be waiting, Tom, right here."

"I can't guarantee anything, Julie. This might take a long time. I expect you to go on. If you meet someone else..."

She interrupted me with a shake of her beautiful head. When she did it, there were tears on her cheeks, and her eyes were closed. She acted as if the words I said--and was about to say--were visible things that she refused to look at.

When she did open her eyes, the last thing she said was, "I'll be here, Tom. No matter what you say, I'll be here...for as long as it takes."

Chapter 21

For much of the four-day drive to Maine, my mind was in a quagmire. Not only did I keep chastising myself for making love to Julie that one time, but I constantly weighed my longing for Julie against the loss of Elaina. With every mile the Subaru ate up, I hurt more for leaving Julie, yet I believed all the more I was doing the right thing as far as Elaina was concerned. Despite all the uncertainty and confusion sloshing around in my head, one realization continually rose to the surface--there were now two holes in my heart, and I couldn't go back to Julie until, if and when, the other one began to heal.

With my emotions in such a tight tangle, I desperately *needed* to go to Maine. I needed time. I also needed to stay alive, but I questioned that need because it was so doubtful I'd ever be able to live a normal life again, no matter where I was. I supposed the only thing keeping me going was the deep-rooted, instinctual, human desire to survive. But I questioned that also. Some of us eventually lose that drive, and I knew I'd already come close to losing mine in that Florida rest stop six months earlier.

The twenty-eight-hundred-mile drive to Bangor was, for the most part, uneventful, which was fine by me. It was near impossible for any Soles haters to recognize me in my new car with the dark windows. Whenever I got out for gas, coffee, or food, I kept my sunglasses on and pulled my brown cap low enough to meet them. Once inside gas stations, truck stops, takeout restaurants, or motel lobbies, I tried to be as inconspicuous as possible, without coming across as peculiar. But something occurred on the second night of the trip that could seriously jeopardize my anonymity.

Solace and I were in a Motel 6 outside of Minneapolis; both of us road weary; lying on a bed, nibbling on pretzels. I'd already taken a shower and was doing my nightly Soleswatch checkup on the laptop. The screen still showed my last spotting in Missoula, but there was a new addition to the five sketches of me. It was photograph of me with Solace, outside the camper, on Julie's property. I knew a telescopic lens had been used to take it because our faces were uncomfortably clear, and the snapshot had been taken from the direction of the river. Since I'd always backed the camper right up to the water, I knew the shot had been taken from the woods beyond.

I also knew perfectly well who took it. And now, by exposing Solace, he'd made it far more difficult for me to remain unrecognizable.

I saw a handful of *Enough is Enough* bumper stickers along the way, all of them near the bigger Midwestern cities and in the Northeast. All of them were worn and faded, but that was no surprise. The social movement my book ignited had cooled drastically after the major retailers nixed it. After that, the movement all but died when Broadstreet International removed it from their lineup. There had been a slight uptick when Denise Solchow's new publishing house put the book out in paperback, but that was confined to a few small groups protesting; waving paperbacks in front of a handful of big chain bookstores. Of course, in those isolated incidents, the folks demonstrating were quickly dispersed by local police.

As I headed east along Interstate 90 and 94, I witnessed various degrees of road rage on several occasions. One time, outside of Chicago, two young hotheads were so enraged they tore off a highway exit together. With only inches separating their bumpers they were obviously on their way to settling their differences. As I watched them make their chancy, speeding exit, I wondered if they'd square things away the old-fashioned way--with fists, or did one or both of them have other ideas. Had they not jerked their vehicles off the Interstate so precariously, I would have followed them to intercede. I'd had more than my share of fights as a young man; and win or lose, there was never anything glorious about two human beings pummeling each other. No rational man on the planet *wants* to fight.

Down the road, when my concern for the two boys in Chicago began to wane, I got to thinking about something other than Elaina and Julie for a change. I thought how for thirty years I'd witnessed a profound change in the attitudes of the American people. As times had gotten harder, so had their demeanors. Road rage, violent crime, divorce rates, pre-nuptial agreements, a fading sense of community—the far-reaching effects of financial difficulties had been boundless. I supposed, as I always had, that our societal devastation was an unfortunate human reflex to the relentless climb of stock market indexes.

The corporate mission to raise share values--ten, fifteen, twenty percent and more, every year--had taken its toll on the American working class. They were the ones who paid most dearly for those increases. The elimination of pensions, union busting, skyrocketing prices, cheapened products, false inflation, and a thousand other profit-driven reasons were why people had become so callous. But the little guy and gal couldn't help it. Again, toughening up was a natural reflex. I knew that if a man or woman had still been paid enough to raise a family, and they had just a few dollars extra to put away at month's end, this country never would have devolved into such a hostile, me-me place.

When I reached that point in my musings, I forced my mind into a different direction. I could no longer worry about such things. When I wrote my book, I'd put those and many more thoughts and observations into it, and look where they had gotten me. Now I had more personal concerns to deal with--far more dangerous concerns.

Nevertheless, Solace and I forged on. By early afternoon of day four, beneath a disheartening gray sky, we passed through Portsmouth, New Hampshire. There's only a short stretch of I-95 passing through that small section of the state, and when you reach the middle of the Piscataqua River Bridge on the north end you enter the state of Maine. For many years there has been a heated dispute over whether the middle of the river or the Maine shoreline should be the border. As I drove through Portsmouth, approaching the bridge, that border reignited yet another dispute--the Elaina/Julie dilemma going on inside my head.

Knowing Julie was from Portsmouth; seeing the city now; being there, made me feel every bit as bad as when I drove away from her standing in front of her cabin that past Monday. Also, with the bridge right there in front of my eyes and the Maine border up at the top, I remembered all too clearly how excited Elaina and I had been each time we'd crossed it together. That recollection came close to reincarnating the indescribable pain I'd felt the day she was shot dead. By the time I reached the border, I was all choked up, and I just wanted it all to end. My vision clouded, engulfed in misery, I really thought my sixty-year-old heart was going to give out. And I did not care.

But a funny thing happened when I got over that bridge. The exact moment my front wheels touched the highway in Maine--that instant--the sun broke through all the gray gloom. The bright light felt ever so soothing as it shone through the windshield. Somehow it washed away all the hurt, despair, and confusion from my face. In the sun's warmth, I felt the tenseness leave and my muscles relax. This new light allowed the towering pines alongside the highway to reclaim their vibrant green color as the clouds parted and new blue hope spread in the sky. Suddenly, the world didn't seem to be such a mean-spirited place.

Stretching my arm back between the seats, I lovingly placed my hand on the brass urn carefully propped on the floor with pillows. I held onto it for a few moments, massaged it, and then I smiled.

Chapter 22

The first two nights in Bangor, Solace and I stayed at the Motel 6. During the days, we drove all over the outskirts of "The Queen City" looking for a rental but had absolutely no luck. There were enough homes and trailers available, but nobody wanted to rent short-term. I'd hoped to find a secluded place and just stay a month or two until I found something to buy. No way was I going to stay in a motel for that period of time. I was comfortable enough those first nights but still uneasy about being in town.

In the late afternoon of the second day, when I was just about to head back to the motel, I saw a dirt road off to my left. We were in a cozy little rural town fourteen miles west of Bangor called Carmel. Solace was as bushed and disgusted as I was and getting very antsy. She'd lie down in her seat, but every few minutes she'd pop back up on all fours and twirl around a few times. I'd been through that drill before and well knew what it meant. I promised her this road would be the last we'd check out.

Like most of the other roads we'd been on in Carmel, this one was nestled in tall pines. All the homes sat on a couple of acres or more, and behind them were thick woods instead of neighbors. It seemed perfect, for the time being. Anyway, just before we reached the end of the road, there was a "For Rent" sign next to a driveway up ahead. With all the brush and trees in front, I couldn't see the place until we reached the driveway. It was a single-wide mobile home; old but tidy, sitting in an absolutely beautiful, park-like setting. It had a nice-sized front lawn and a slightly larger grassy area in back--from what I could see of that. I couldn't see a neighbor in any direction, just woods. After walking around the empty place, I went back to the sign out front, with my cell, and called the owner.

When I mentioned the short-term catch, he paused on the other end, but then he said he'd be over in ten minutes. Full of hope now, with Solace on her leash, I went to the back again and stepped into the woods a short ways. Being early May, it was still cool, and cooler yet in the shadows of the trees. As I walked along the forest floor, dead leaves and winter fallen branches cracking and crunching beneath my sneakers, I ruminated about my immediate plans.

From the short periods of time Elaina and I had stayed in the Bangor area over the years, I still didn't know if the outlying areas were isolated enough to settle down in. When we'd gone there in the past, we hadn't explored the areas to the north, which was my present plan. I could push another two hours north and look around Presque Isle, where I knew there were plenty of secluded areas. But just as the landlord pulled up in the driveway, setting Solace off immediately, I decided if north of Bangor wasn't right for me I could still operate out of this trailer. From time to time, I could drive farther upstate; grab a motel room in different areas; explore for a couple of days; then come back and relax for a while.

The owner of the trailer was close to my age, a bit shorter and a real outdoorsy, can-do kind of guy. Not only that, but he turned out to be one of the finest human beings I'd ever met. It was about fifty degrees the day a jacketless Gary Cyrus first extended his hand to me, but he looked perfectly comfortable in just a tee shirt that was black as his hair. He looked like the type of man who could lose himself in the woods and survive with just the Swiss Army knife holstered on the belt that held up his jeans.

After taking a look inside the trailer and talking things over, he gladly rented me the place at a more than fair fee. After telling the fifth generation Mainer that I'd like to move in as soon as possible; that I'd just pick up a few pieces of used furniture to get by with; he wouldn't stand for it. Gary said he had an extra twin bed at his place and an upholstered chair and a few other things he could bring right over, if I wanted to move in right then. When I told them that would be terrific, that I could shoot back to the motel and pick up my things, he said that was fine. But he also said that I looked like I could use a cold beer first. I could have kissed him on the forehead at that point, instead, I just said "sure." He went to his pickup truck, brought back a small cooler with a six-pack on ice, and we split it on the back porch steps.

As planned, we stayed at Gary's trailer for two full months. And at least once a week he'd come over with his six-pack, and we'd sit out on the porch. I always had my own beer in the refrigerator, but he always insisted we drink his. We quickly became good friends, and every time we knocked off his sixer, we'd grab a few more from my stock. I really enjoyed his company, and every time he left, I thought what a better world it would be if everyone had a bit of Gary Cyrus in them.

Our stay in Carmel was very peaceful and without incident, but I still kept an eye on Soleswatch. I couldn't do that from the trailer because I never had the phone service turned on. So every now and then I'd drive over to a certain motel in Bangor, park in back, and check out the latest developments using their Wi-Fi and my laptop. As far as the site's followers knew, I was still in Missoula.

The only other times I ever left Carmel were to make four trips upstate. After quickly deciding that outside the Bangor area wasn't isolated enough for me, I knew I'd have to push north. On only the second trip, I was lucky enough to find a suitable mobile home in an out-of-the-way place called White Pine. I bought it for just the past due taxes and legal fees, which were next to nothing. There was very little demand for housing in White Pine, and the price of what little real estate was for sale reflected that. With a population of only 452 hardy souls spread over nineteen square miles, and most of the young people migrating to bigger cities as soon as they could, it wasn't what you'd call a boom town. If a homeowner decided to move away from White Pine, or mysteriously vanished like Norm Flagg, the trailer's previous owner had, there surely wouldn't be any bidding wars going on.

It seemed like the perfect place for Solace and me. Sitting on ten acres of land, it backed on, and faced, nothing but dense forest. The trailer was set up in the trees much the same way as the one in Carmel but with a bigger front and back yard. The long dirt road leading up to it was in horrendous shape, and I figured that could only add to my sense of security. Not only were there ruts and deep holes everywhere, but it was uneven, as well. This was not a road anyone would use unless they absolutely had to. Another plus was that the closest neighbors were about two miles away, at the very beginning of what they call Split Branch Road. And I was at the far end of it. A fugitive like me couldn't have asked for a better spot to hole up. In early July I closed on the property and furnished it with things from a Salvation Army store in Presque Isle.

For the first eleven months here in White Pine, Solace and I kept totally to ourselves. I did phone Julie every week and Gary Cyrus a few times. Denise Solchow, my editor, called me from time to time, too. She not only kept me up to date on the diminishing sales of *Enough is Enough*, but she'd been kind enough to buy books for me to read. Her sending them here was a life saver, since the only stores in White Pine were a gas station/general store and a place called Edna's Country Café. I'm sure the closest things to literature they carry were *The Bangor Daily News* and a handful of magazines. Even if they had more books than Barnes and Noble, I couldn't patronize them. I had to stay out of public places for fear of losing my anonymity and the peace of mind it allowed me.

That first summer we had warmer weather than normal. Most mornings I drove to a nearby logging road that was no longer in use and jogged a few miles. I also had my reading to keep me occupied, the computer, and Lord knows, plenty of yard work. Solace and I both loved the property and spent much of our time relaxing on the back porch. I sipped coffee out there in the mornings, and in the afternoons, at about three, we'd go out there again. I'd nurse a few beers, and both us would just take it easy and keep an eye out for the wildlife. Of course, we saw far more animals during the morning shifts. One early morning when we'd first moved in, we were allowed a very special treat. Before we'd gone out, while waiting for the coffee to brew, two winter-battered moose showed up in the backyard. I picked Solace up so she, too, could see out the living room window, and we watched them for a long time. Both the mother and daughter were huge but very, very thin. Their coats pale and rough, they alternated nibbles on the new grass with occasional glances at us.

Every morning we had close to twenty wild turkeys show up, also. They loved the cracked corn I sprinkled beneath our bird feeder. But the turkeys weren't nearly as tolerant as the moose had been. We had to stand well behind the kitchen window, and off to the side, to watch them. If they noticed me watching, or if Solace started barking, they were out of there-- like right now. I also loved watching the squirrels, chipmunks, and the rest of the birds that found sanctuary here as well. Solace, on the other hand, would have preferred to go after them had I allowed her. Of all the birds that frequented the backyard, I was most fond of the diminutive hummingbirds. They'd come right up to the two feeders I'd hung from the porch eaves and hover, while we sat right there. After they migrated south in early September I sorely missed them. I truly enjoyed all my feathered and furry neighbors. With them around, I didn't feel quite so alone.

My only face-to-face encounters with human beings were when I made two trips to Carmel to see Gary and on my monthly, fifty-mile supply runs to Presque Isle. During the latter, I'd buy cigarettes, load up on beer, and get my groceries at a small, out-of-the-way grocery store. I'd have loved to buy everything I needed at Ike's General Store, in White Pine, but that would have been too risky. I simply could not let people see my face—especially here. Even though I'd been going by the name of Darius McClure since I arrived, it was all too possible that someone might have recognized me. It was one hell of a way to live, but if I wanted to stay in one place and one piece, that was the only way. Even when I'd rented the trailer in Carmel, from Gary, I had to tell him my name was Tom Ferguson. As I did with Franklin Dewitt in Florida, I often wondered if he knew who I really was.

By the time November rolled around, our pleasurable outdoor activities were all but over. That eleventh month is nobody's favorite in New England. Almost like clockwork, the weather becomes cold and damp, the skies gloomy. Dark, tufted clouds droop low, overhead, like soggy, old, gray upholstery.

And they seem to homestead there. The abysmal weather offers nothing positive for the human spirit's inner flame. By the time November grudgingly came to an end, that fire in my damaged spirit had been all but extinguished. But it was more than just climactic conditions that brought me to those new lows. It was also deer hunting season.

Nary was there a day that a gunshot didn't ring out in the woods. And every blast brought me back that much closer to my last day with Elaina. With each shot, the vision of her dying in my arms became more vivid. Over and over, I felt her body grow cold in my arms; each time my heart ached a little bit more.

Ever since I had lost Elaina that November morning a year earlier, the sun never set on a day that she wasn't near the center of my thoughts. Every time one of those rifle shots pierced my soul, all I could do was retreat to the bedroom. I'd just lay in there staring up at the trailer's low ceiling, oblivious to it, holding Elaina's burgundy cap. Sometimes I stayed in that bed until I cried myself to sleep. Dawn, dusk, the middle of the day, it did not matter. And by the time hunting season finally ended, I didn't look any better than those two haggard moose I'd seen earlier that year. Of course, I couldn't see or feel the spirits of those tired animals, but I know damn well they had been in far better shape than mine were by the end of November.

The Maine winter that followed was frigid and long, but Solace and I handled it quite well. She loved frolicking in the deep snow. She also liked to dig in it, burying her head as she hunted down mice. One time she surfaced from a foot of the white stuff with one in her mouth. I yelled at her to drop it, but that was one of the few times she would not listen to me. I can still visualize that poor wiggling tail sticking out of Solace's mouth as she took it down headfirst. The woodstove in the small living room kept us nice and toasty while inside, and reading certainly helped me pass the time. The books kept coming from Denise, and Manny Ruiz shipped my entire collection from New York along with the few other items I cared to hold onto. I asked Manny if he could sell everything else he'd put in storage for me. I told him he could keep all the proceeds, and though he thought it wasn't fair that he should keep all the money, I managed to persuade him. I also settled a couple of other affairs.

With my countrywide ramblings hopefully behind me, living much cheaper now, I tried to figure out how much money I'd need for the future. Just in case I actually had one. After adding in the social security I'd begin collecting in one year, I kept just enough to get by on. Then, on one of my trips to Presque Isle, I went to the bank and finally had $758,000.00 sent to Habitat for Humanity.

When at long last spring arrived, I could feel my mangled spirits rising along with the temperatures. No longer did it get dark outside at three-thirty in the afternoon. The cracks I'd gotten in my fingertips from the cold began to heal. What was left of the biggest snowdrifts was small and scattered. Velvety pussy willows bloomed up and down Split Branch Road, and green buds appeared on the limbs of the few maples and elms on the property. I could hear the stream in the woods across the road flowing again. A layer of thin grass began to sprout in the front and back, and I no longer needed my navy-blue sock hat or insulated jacket.

Happily, I resumed my jogging on the logging roads. As I ran each morning with the sun warm on my face, I began to feel a little more at peace with my loss of Elaina. Of course, the passage of time had also helped the healing process. Like Julie had said, and I knew, Elaina would always be with me. But still, I was doing a somewhat better job of handling the dark void that still lurked inside me. Julie and I still talked every week, and we missed each other terribly. She never hounded me to come back to her, but it was more than obvious she wanted that badly. Nevertheless, all things considered, I was feeling considerably better. Of course, I was fed up with hiding out like a criminal. And there were times I questioned whether such an existence was better than the alternative. But in spite of that uncertainty, I actually felt a little bounce returning to my step.

Then things got even better. One bright sunny day at the end of May I became friends with my mailman. I'd rather not go into the details of what brought on our first conversation, so let's just say I was hanging from a tree limb thirty feet off the ground, and he saved me. The important point is that I made a friend. Take it from me--it is not healthy to go months on end without trading any words of consequence with another human being. Sure, I'd talked to Solace plenty, but they were always one-sided conversations. There were the phone calls, too, but they were few and far between. As much as I'd lost faith in humanity, I was still a part of that questionable lot. I still needed to exchange thoughts and feelings with somebody. Jake Snow was just the person I needed.

Twenty years younger than I, Jake turned out to be a very caring, insightful person. And that was lucky for me. Not thinking rationally the day he saved me from that impending fall, I invited him into the trailer for a beer. Normally that would have been perfectly fine, but Jake, like everybody else in White Pine, thought my name was Darius McClure. Shook up as I was from my near demise, I'd completely forgotten about a newspaper article I'd hung on the living room wall. Framed and in plain view was the front page of The New York Times with a picture of me accepting The Nobel Prize. And the caption beneath it certainly didn't state my name as Darius McClure. If Jake Snow hadn't turned out to be such a prince I would have certainly blown my cover.

With the sun shining through the living room window that afternoon, we had a long talk. Slowly sipping beer in reclining chairs, we spoke of much bigger things than new acquaintances usually do. Nevertheless, starved as I was for human interaction, I was wary at first. I had to be. But that quickly changed. In no time at all I realized I wasn't only talking to a man with an affable personality but a deep sense of integrity as well. There was no question about it--Jake was a no-nonsense, straight-from-the-heart, forthright man. So when I opened up to him, far sooner than I normally would under such circumstances, it felt perfectly natural. And that was fine. Jake was very interested in everything I told him. It seemed he couldn't get enough of my stories.

That's why, when it came time for him to leave, I asked if he'd like to read my memoir. I deeply wanted to share my unfortunate experiences with someone I could trust. I *needed* to share them. There is nothing in this world, other than the passage of time that can help heal wounds like heartfelt empathy from another. It is truly amazing how releasing pent-up troubles can actually lighten them.

Another thing I knew for sure was: I'd be damn thankful for any help I could muster after a year and a half on the run. Though I had come to love Julie at the end of my Montana stay, I hadn't wanted to overload her with every last detail at once. And I felt the same way about Jake. I told him I'd give him just one chapter every week to read. I also told him if he got to a point where he felt he was learning things that he shouldn't know, information that could put him at risk, he should stop reading right then and there.

When Jake returned a chapter each week, usually on Saturdays, we'd share a few beers and talk. We'd discussed what he'd most recently read and then go onto other things. A few times he told me how rising prices were weighing down on his spirit. How the constant skyrocketing costs of gasoline, food, and health insurance were making a shambles of his budget. But for the most part, we discussed broader issues. We talked about America's drowning working class, the environment, the wars cropping up all around the globe, and the devolving human condition. We looked to each other for hope and optimism. And though we had to dig deep sometimes, we did find glints of both. As the weeks stacked into months, our talks and my recorded words brought Jake and me closer and closer. All through the summer and into the fall our fondness for each other only grew.

By the end of October, it felt as if Jake Snow was the son I never had, and I think he considered me his mentor. Between our close relationship and the anonymity I'd been able to hold onto in White Pine, I could feel my healing process accelerating. For the first time since Elaina and I returned from Stockholm, a few soothing rays of hope were finding their way into my spirit.

Then everything went all to hell again.

Chapter 23

Right after Jake finished reading the last completed chapter of my memoir, some strange, unnerving events started taking place. The first occurred one dreary afternoon when I was out back on the rider mower; mulching the last of autumn's fallen leaves. Low, sallow clouds seemed to rest atop the pines, and there was a damp nip in the northeast wind. Solace was lazing on the porch, wishing she could come out by me, when she suddenly started some serious barking. It wasn't a let-me-out-with-you-Tom kind of bark. It was angry and aggressive. Every bit as agitated as she'd been when we once saw a fisher chase a squirrel around the shed, she was again trying to climb up and through the screen door. I yelled at her to stop scratching, but she wouldn't listen.

Knowing for sure now that something was up, I quickly drove the rider to the end of the trailer. Stopping there I peered around the Subaru and down the driveway. Sure enough, about a minute and a half later--the time it takes to reach the end of the road, make a u-turn, and come back again--a huge, muscular pickup truck slowed to a stop at the end of my drive. It was one of those fifty-thousand-dollar models, a shiny black Ford F-450 with dual wheels in the back. The type you almost need a ladder to climb up into. This truck's presence may not seem like enough reason for alarm, but other than Jake's jeep, the garbage truck, and the snowplow, not a single soul had driven by my place in the sixteen months I'd been there. As I said earlier, nobody without a damn good reason drives to the far end of Split Branch Road. It's that bad.

I gestured a hello, but whoever was inside did not open the tinted windows. As I slowly dropped my hand to my side, a very eerie feeling slipped over me. I felt susceptible, defenseless. The hair on my arms stood up like the fur on a scared cat's back.

Staring at the black glass for a moment, wondering who and what motives were on the other side, I considered going inside for the Glock. Instead I started walking toward the truck. And as soon as I did, the over-sized Ford started to roll forward. An instant later, I lost sight of it behind the thick trees buffering the front lawn from the road, and I broke into an all-out run like a sprinter who'd heard a starting gun go off. I wanted to see what kind of plates were on that truck. Maybe I could get the number, just in case. With the poor condition of the road I knew he'd never make it out of sight without my being able to see the rear plate.

When I reached the road, the hulking truck was farther along than I thought it would be. Bouncing and jouncing like a runaway maverick, the driver was really pushing it. But I could still see the back bumper, and there was no license plate.

Head down and deflated, I trudged back toward the trailer. As I made my way across the withered brown lawn, an entire swarm of frenzied thoughts spun wildly in my mind. They were disheartening thoughts, each a revitalized fear--stinging hard at the sense of well-being I'd so carefully fostered since coming to White Pine. I wondered why in God's name things had to be the way they were. This life business is difficult enough to begin with. Some go so far as to speculate that the time we spend on earth is in actuality both heaven and hell. While there is no sure way of knowing this, I did know one thing for certain. I'd had more than my share of living hell.

Once inside the trailer, I opened the back door to let Solace in from the porch. I then grabbed a beer, drug feet into the living room, and flopped into my recliner. With shaking hands, the paneled walls feeling like they were closing in on me, I lit a cigarette.

Jesus no, not again!, I thought. *What in the hell am I going to do now? All these months of relative peace, and now this. What was he, or they, doing here? I don't even know how many were in the truck. No...I don't know that, but I sure as hell do know somebody went through the trouble of taking that plate off for a reason. There's an agenda behind all this. Either somebody or some people are just trying to shake me up a little, let me know they're not real happy about my being here, or they have far more serious plans. They very well could have been*

*surveilling the place to make sure I am who they suspect. Then
what? What's next? Fuck...this isn't pretty!*

Two beers later, I decided I was not going to just up and
leave this time. I had a home now, not just an RV. It would
take more than just some angry cretin to drive me away. Things
would have to get far worse. Not only that, but if whoever was
in that truck came back again, and they brought with them more
serious intentions, I'd be ready for them. I may be an emotional,
peaceable person, but I was sick of it all and was not going to
take this kind of crap lying down anymore. Before that
devastating afternoon that Elaina and I returned from Sweden, I
had never let anyone walk all over me. Now I'd had it. It
wasn't going to happen again. Sure, I was scared. Once again, I
could taste fear's vile bitterness, but this time I wasn't going to
swallow it. I was ready to spit it out and fight for whatever I
had to.

Though the weather was turning, it still wasn't too cold to
jog the logging road. All bundled up in a sweatshirt and the
Bean jacket, with the sock hat back on my head, I went late the
following morning. More than a little paranoid, my windblown
eyes constantly scoured the trees on both sides of the deserted,
narrow road. I also watched up ahead and turned around toward
the Subaru often. Solace was in it. She never had the stamina to
go the three miles with me, so I'd always left her at home. Now
I refused to. I also didn't like her being a mile and a half away
by the time I turned to head back. But bringing her along
seemed like the safest precautionary option. And everything
went smoothly that first day.

The next day I decided to run only three-quarters of a mile
beyond the Subaru; then turn around and head back. When I
reached the car again, I'd proceed the same distance in the
opposite direction. This way, after the first half of the run, if
anybody came up the logging road, I'd see them coming and at
least not have to worry about Solace. Plus, I'd never be more
than three-fourths of a mile away from her. Though I felt
awfully foolish for not thinking of this strategy the day before, I
blamed it on the findings of another Nobel Prize recipient. After
months of jogging this road, always doing it the same way, I'd

been conditioned like one of Ivan Pavlov's dogs. Nevertheless, I was very relieved not to be so far away from my own dog.

Jogging the first leg at a faster clip than usual so I'd get back quicker, I kept looking over my shoulder, making sure everything was okay. Then, when I took the very last look before hitting my new turnaround point, I saw something coming up the road. Raising dust in the distance there was a vehicle--making its way toward the Subaru. Though it was far away, and bright sunlight reflecting from its windshield made it difficult to see, it looked like a truck, and it looked black.

Instantly, I spun around and broke into an all-out run. Already breathing hard from the accelerated pace, I pumped my knees and fists as high and fast as I possibly could. My strides were long and my focus did not leave that vehicle. Soon my lungs were burning. So were the straining muscles in my legs as I pushed on. Feeling for the all but useless bear-mace holstered at my side, wishing it was the Glock, my heart pummeled inside its ribbed cage like the fist of a crazed gorilla. Cold as it was, in the mid-thirties, I felt perspiration rising on my forehead beneath the sock hat. The trees enveloping me on both sides of the road blurred green in my periphery, but my eyes, wrenching as if in pain, bore straight ahead.

Half the way back by now, there was no longer any question. Slowing down behind my car, towering behind it like an ominous black storm cloud, was the same Ford that had stopped in front of my driveway. I couldn't yet hear Solace's barks but knew she had to be going absolutely crazy. I was. It didn't matter if the son-of-a-bitch shot me dead, I was going to do anything I could to protect Solace. I couldn't make out his features or even tell if he was wearing a hat, but I did see somebody lean out the driver's side window. Then, a few strides later, there was a shot.

I flinched but kept running--harder now. As if it were rocket fuel, a new dose of adrenaline rushed through my limbs, propelling me even faster. I started weaving--zigging and zagging like an all-star running back. Sure, the bastard might hit me, but I wasn't going to be a sitting duck.

As I closed in on the truck, close enough now to hear Solace's desperate barks--maybe a hundred and fifty yards away--I couldn't believe my terrorized eyes. Not slowing down a bit, my chest totally in flames now, the truck started to move. The driver goosed the gas and the big rig lunged sharply to its left. He was actually making a u-turn. With the size of the pickup and the narrowness of the road it was a five-point-turn instead of a three, but it was a u-turn. And when he completed it, he took off so fast the dirt and stones his four rear tires peeled backwards peppered my Subaru like debris in a Category-5 hurricane. I could just imagine Solace inside, clawing at the glass, going even more psycho than before, as the stones pinged and dinged the back of the car.

Finally, the truck's tires made better traction, and it hauled back down that road as if it was at Daytona. I slowed to a rapid walk, grabbed my sides, and struggled for every breath. With my heart still thumping harder and faster than it had a right to, I watched the Ford quickly shrink in the distance. Somehow, I quelled the urge to chase it down. Like I said, my pistol was in the glove box. I could have gone after the truck, tried to put an end to all this lunacy one way or another. But I didn't. Whoever was in that Ford was toying with me. He could have ended me right there and then. I didn't know if that was his ultimate intention, or he wasn't quite crazy enough to go that far. There were a lot of blanks to be filled in and questions to be answered. But I did know one thing for sure, there was no doubt in my mind that I hadn't seen the last of that truck.

When I got home twenty minutes later, I entered the trailer Glock first. Like a detective entering the home of a dangerous felon, I crouched low while peeking in the doorways to all the rooms. After finishing a thorough investigation--under the beds, inside the closets, behind the recliners--I may have felt a little foolish, but this was far from a joking matter. For two years I'd been living like a runaway slave, and now I'd finally had it. Sure, the months in White Pine had been peaceful, but all that time I'd been forced to live like a scared animal in a burrow. Bad as that existence had been, I'd made the best of it. Now, even that was over.

The only two options left were to put the gun to my head or come up with yet another plan. I didn't know what the right thing to do was. Not having a clue, I rushed into the bedroom, picked up Elaina's urn from the dresser, lay down in bed with it, and only hoped she could give me guidance.

After a long, long time in that bedroom, I'd finally devised a plan. I didn't know if there was enough time to enact it, but it was my only chance. After working out the very last detail, I kissed the urn and placed it back on the dresser. Then there was a knock at the front door.

I picked up the pistol, tried unsuccessfully to quiet Solace down, then made my way to the living room and peeked out the window. It was Jake Snow.

"Whew," I said, "hello Jake. Come on in."

"Holy God, what's going on, Tom?" he asked, after he slid in the doorway and saw my face and the gun in my hand. "What's wrong? You look terrible, like you've seen a closet full of ghosts."

Extending my hand toward the chairs, I asked him to have a seat.

We both sat down, and after I rubbed my forehead a few times, I told him, "Things are not good, Jake." Then I filled him in on everything, beginning with the truck stopping outside the driveway. By the time I finished, the concern on Jake's face had deepened and he said, "Damn it, Tom, I hate like hell to have to tell you this, but I have some more bad news. Take a look at this. It's the only mail I've got for you today."

He then handed me a post card; a plain white post card. Atop of my address on the front, scrawled in red ink, it read, Mr. Thomas Soles c/o Darius McClure.

Immediately, a mortifying sense of doom dropped over me like an immovable steel net. The realization that I had been found again, and all the consequences that would surely follow, were undeniable now.

"Son of a bitch," I said, sitting there, staring at the card. Then I turned it over. In all caps it said, LEAVE OR DIE!

This wasn't a request. It was yet another demand. My life was all but over. In a skipped heartbeat, the few scraps of hope

I'd had left evacuated my soul. At that moment, I knew I'd never again experience the peace of mind a sense of normalcy allows. For as long as I might go on, no matter where I flee to, if I was to live at all, it would always be minute to minute. Although I'd been forced to make many painful concessions, I'd at least been fortunate enough to flirt with contentment while in White Pine. Even that had been a tremendous relief after what I'd lived through. Now even that was gone.

I laid the postcard on the table between Jake and me and just looked at him. There wasn't a lot either of us could say as the thrust of devastation and helplessness sank deeper inside us both.

After a moment or two of disturbed silence, Jake drew a long breath. As he let it out his eyes rose slowly. I don't know if he was looking at the pines and blue sky outside the window or the Times article hanging alongside it, but he said, "What the fuck is wrong with people, Tom? All you ever did was tried to help. You shed some light on all the unfairness out there--let people know just how royal a screwing they're getting—and what happens? You get *death* threats!"

"Unfortunately, Jake, there are people in this world who love their misbegotten wealth far more than anything else. Right or wrong doesn't matter to them. If they feel their fortunes are being threatened in any way, more than a few of them would kill to protect their stashes. Do you think my life means a damn thing to people like that?"

"It certainly doesn't seem it does to the son of a bitch who sent you that card. Christ, Tom…what're you going to do?"

"Listen closely," I said, "Before we get into all that, I need to tell you a few things…things that are very important to me."

"Sure, go ahead. I'm all ears," he said. But the tone of his voice told me he was having trouble dismissing his anger.

"Please, forget about all that for now. Let it go for just a few minutes, Jake."

"Alright, alright. Sorry. Go ahead."

"I'd like to give you a key to the place, in case something happens to me. If it does, I'd like for you to send my manuscript to Denise Solchow, my publisher in New York. Would you do that for me, Jake?"

"Hell, I don't want to hear this stuff. But yeah, of course I will."

"Okay," I said, tapping a cigarette out of the pack on the table, just fumbling with it as I went on. "The hardcopy you've read will be on the top shelf in the bedroom closet. As you know, it's not quite finished yet. The laptop over there," I said, pointing to where it sat on the sofa to our right, "that one's up to date. As a matter of fact, I'm writing in the present now. All of it has been in retrospect, but now it's up to date. What will go into it next is as much a mystery to me as it will be to whoever might read it."

With resent and resignation hanging from all his words now, Jake rushed them out as if they were soil on his tongue, "Yeah, okay Tom. Where's her address, your publisher?"

"They're in the closet, too; on top of the manuscript. If the one in the computer isn't complete, send them both to her anyway. Okay?"

"No problem," he said.

I then lit the cigarette, drew on it, and went on. "Alright then, there are two more things. One I have to ask you and the other I have to tell you. First, if something does happen, will you take care of Solace for me?"

Without hesitation he started to say, "Sure, I..." But I held up my hand and interrupted him.

"I know she's a difficult animal. She has her issues. If you don't think you could handle her with the kids and all at home, just try to find her a good home. That in itself wouldn't be easy, but please try. You know her now. You know that beneath all that aggression and..."

Now it was Jake's turn to interrupt, "Forget it, Tom. Don't give it a thought. Solace would stay with us. That's something you never have to worry about. Now, what did you want to tell me? I'd rather get on to something else, like what you're planning to do next."

Relieved that that was resolved, I stubbed out my cigarette in the glass ashtray, swished it around a few times, and looked back at my friend. "Jake," I said, "I know you're not going to like this, but just hear me out, alright?"

"I'm listening."

"I've put in my will, which, by the way, is in a metal box next to the manuscript, that if I should pass on, the trailer and property will be yours."

"No, no, no!" he said, straightening up in his chair, looking at me as if I'd done something totally irrational. "I could never accept…"

"Yes you could, Jake. I have no heirs in waiting. There are no kids, no…no wife, there's nobody."

"You could leave it to a charity."

"I've done a lot for charities already. If the memoir ever takes off, all the royalties would go to charities also. It's tough out there, Jake. There would be nothing wrong with you and your family receiving a small windfall. You could do whatever you want with the place, sell it, rent it, that's up to you. My concern is that you have a little something behind you because, and mark my words, as bad as things are they're probably going to get worse."

Hunching over on the edge of his recliner now, elbows to his knees but still looking straight at me, he said in a resigned tone, "That's damn nice of you, Tom. Okay. Thank you. Thank you very much. But let's not talk about this anymore, alright? Can we move on to your plans now?"

And that is what we did. We talked about my next move, which was to just sit and wait. I'd decided not to run anymore. Cold as it was getting, there would be no more jogging for me. I'd go on like I had been. I'd dig in for the winter and only leave the trailer for my monthly supply runs. Whatever would happen would happen. I'd keep the Glock close by and not think twice about using it if I had to. And it looked like I would, because just before Jake left, we checked the Soleswatch tracker page. A new update showed I was in White Pine, Maine, driving around in a maroon Subaru. It had been posted only an hour earlier.

That night, lying in bed with all my fears and dead hopes, I called Julie Dubois. I did not beat around the bush. Like I had with Jake, I told her everything that had happened. I told Julie we could never be together again, and that the time had come for her to look for somebody else. She argued and argued, but I wouldn't relent. My life story may be destined to a cruel, premature end, but there was no way in hell I was going to let it happen to hers. Lying there in the darkness, I eviscerated both our hearts with that cell phone. But it could be no other way. I had to be firm. I was not going to endanger her life, or tie it up any more. But Julie was Julie. Sweet as she is, she could be every bit as firm as the age-old mountains alongside her cabin. Her last words were the very same ones she used when I left her in Montana that day. Again she insisted, "I'll be here, Tom…for as long as it takes."

Chapter 24

As I write this today, the first snowfall of the year seems to be coming to an end. The afternoon sky is still gray, but everything beneath it is coated white and this small piece of the world looks so pristine. The wind has let up, and the hush outside is only interrupted by a solitary chickadee at the birdfeeder. It keeps calling out the name of its species as it seeks out its friends. *Chick-a-dee-dee-dee, chick-a-dee-dee-dee*, it calls over and over. As I sit here typing these words, I can only envy the small bird. How I wish I, too, could mingle with my kind. Oh, sure, I'd be particularly choosy about whom I associated with in this jaded twenty-first century, but I wouldn't have to hide anymore. Unfortunately, I am who I am, and circumstances in my life do not permit me to interact with the rest of this planet's inhabitants. All I can hope is that this memoir will go to print, and that some readers will be enraged at the price I've paid for speaking out. Please forgive me. When I sat down to write today I hadn't intended to get into all this. I am sorry. It's just that that bird outside has led my thoughts in a melancholic direction. It's time to turn them around. Such musings could be harmful to someone in my delicate condition. All I can do is remain vigilant and fight to steer my thinking away from such emotions.

It's now been five days since that gun went off on the logging road. Nobody has come up Split Branch Road, and there haven't been any incidents since. Yesterday, I had to make a trip down to Presque Isle, but that went as smoothly as I could hope. I brought Solace with me this time. I wasn't about to leave her here, alone. At both the stores I went to, I parked as close to the front doors as possible. Once inside, I kept checking out the windows, making sure she was okay. Had anybody been watching me, they'd have surely thought I was more than a little peculiar. Despite all my covert efforts, particularly with my dark glasses on and watch-cap pulled low, I must have looked like a hyped-up bank robber who'd just passed a note to a teller.

Other than that trip, and when Jake has stopped over for a few minutes, these past days have been filled with an endless stream of fear and depression. As I wait and wonder if each day will be my last, I feel like an imprisoned man awaiting his turn at the gallows. It's again becoming increasingly difficult to ward off thoughts of suicide. Every morning, when I wake up, that option seems a little more viable. Is it better to sit here waiting for my executioner? I'm beginning to think not. On top of all these life and death concerns, I am heartbroken about what I had to tell Julie. When I'm not contemplating my demise, I constantly worry about how my decision is affecting her. What have her days been like since I let her down? How is she coping? Is she coping? Had I totally ruined the life of yet another very special woman? Is it possible she could someday bounce back from this? What is going through her mind this very...Shit, excuse me; Solace has suddenly become highly agitated. She's about to tear down the back door in the kitchen. Something's out there. I have to go see.

* * *

Thomas Soles' memoir ended there. Those last words were written on a Sunday, and since there was no mail delivery, I did not stop over to check on him that day. God knows I wish I had. The date of Tom's disappearance was November 2nd--exactly two years from the day his wife, Elaina, had been shot dead in the Great Smoky Mountains.

When I delivered Tom's mail Monday afternoon, he did not answer the door when I knocked. His Subaru was parked in the driveway, so I went around back to see if he might be out there. But he wasn't. The only thing I found were footprints in the melting snow. One set came out of the woods, from the side of the backyard, leading directly to the porch door. Investigators from Portland said they were a man's size 13. Tom wore an 11. His prints, along with Solaces's paw prints, went from the porch straight to the *back* of the yard and did not continue into the woods because there was no snow cover on the forest floor. Just behind their prints was the size 13's again. The authorities concluded that whoever it was had come out of the trees--on the side of the trailer--and snuck onto the porch. He was obviously armed, and when Tom came out to investigate, the perpetrator ambushed him.

There was no sign of a struggle by the porch, but there was on the far side of the backyard. Right where the snow cover and prints ended at the tree line, there was snow flailed all over. There was also a mixture of both men's footprints as well as paw prints. It was concluded that just before being forced into the woods, surely at gunpoint, Tom grappled with the bigger man. A few drops of blood were found at the scene, and tests proved they were, without a doubt, Tom's.

The investigation lasted eight days. Every law enforcement agency from local constable Curtis Bass to the Maine Bureau of Investigation was involved. The one thing that stumped them all was why the man who'd come for Tom hadn't ended his life right there and then. After all, there wasn't a living soul within two miles of the trailer.

With the help of their dogs, investigators were able to track the threesome's path through the woods for quite some distance. Their trail went about two hundred yards back from the trailer, and then it ran parallel to Split Branch all the way to State Route 5. It is presumed that, at that point, all three got into a waiting vehicle and drove off. To where, nobody has a clue. Were there other people involved, possibly waiting in the getaway vehicle? Nobody can answer that either. Five months have now passed and the general consensus around the globe is that Nobel Laureate Thomas Soles is a dead man.

Though they have since ended, when news of Tom's abduction was first released, there were even more marches and protests than when the book had first made its mark on the world. Denise Solchow has published his memoir, and its sales have already surpassed those of the first book. Since Tom had never given it a title, Denise did. She called it *The Last American Martyr*, and it was released just two weeks after Tom was officially declared dead. The truly ironic thing was that, before the book came out, Broadstreet International did everything they could to get the publishing rights. The same company that had whisked Tom's first book off of so many store shelves, and fired Denise, was down on its pinstriped knees begging and bribing her in every way imaginable. Of course, she wouldn't have anything to do with them.

As for myself, I've been going on the best I can. For these past few months there has been nothing left in my heart but an overwhelming sense of loss. Happiness, hopefulness, even contentment have become alien emotions. My dank spirits hit an all-time low last Tuesday when I finally gave in to one of Tom's last requests. I sprinkled Elaina's ashes amongst the trees behind his trailer--right near where I'd saved him with that ladder. No, I haven't been myself since the moment I found Tom's open laptop sitting on his recliner that day. When I went inside his trailer, after seeing those footprints in the yard and read those last few lines, I knew it was all over. I knew a horrific tragedy had taken place. I knew that not only had I lost my closest friend, but that the world had lost one of its finest inhabitants.

Yes, I was sure of all that, until yesterday afternoon, when my cell phone rang. I had just finished making my last two deliveries, wouldn't you know it, at the beginning of Split Branch Road. It was Tom. He was calling from somewhere in Alaska. He didn't tell me exactly where, and I know well and good why he didn't. It had more to do with preserving my safety than it did his own. At any rate, he did tell me that he was up there with Julie Dubois. They had bought, in her name, a small homestead in a remote part of the forty-ninth state. He told me that she had sold her Montana place before they enacted Tom's plan. Yes, that's what his disappearance had been—a plan. For the last few months he'd been here in his trailer, Tom and Julie had been working out all the details during their phone conversations. Then, on November 2nd, three days after Julie had driven her pickup truck all the way from Missoula to Maine, they enacted those plans.

After Julie spent two days in a Bangor motel room and a third in Millinocket--waiting for that first snowfall--Tom called her and told her to head up here. As soon as he hung up the phone, with close to the predicted four inches on the ground, Tom went to work.

First he put on a pair of second-hand, size 13 boots he'd bought in Presque Isle. Then, leaving Solace in the trailer, he went out on the back porch, picked up several slabs of firewood for added weight, and headed for the woods beyond his yard. Once there, with those tracks behind him, he walked through the pines to the side of the yard and left another trail leading *to the porch*. After putting the wood back on his pile, he went inside and got Solace leashed up. They then walked back toward the tree line, alongside the first set of tracks, so it appeared the owner of the larger boots had coaxed Tom at gunpoint. Just before they stepped out of the yard and onto the forest floor, Tom kicked up and stomped some snow to simulate a struggle. He then cut his thumb with a Swiss army knife and scattered a few drops of blood.

After that the rest was easy. There was virtually no snow in the woods, so with Solace on the leash, the two extra boots in his other hand, and his gold Nobel medal in his pocket, the two of them made good time all the way to Route 5. Tom's only fear was that before reaching his and Julie's rendezvous spot, he or Solace might get nailed by a careless deer hunter's bullet. But that didn't happen. And it was only a matter of minutes after reaching deserted Route 5 that Tom was in Julie's truck and in her arms.

Just before Tom and I hung up our phones, right after he promised to call back soon, I asked him how he was holding up.

He said, "Jake, for the first time in a very long time I can honestly say I'm glad to be alive."

The End

188

CPSIA information can be obtained at www.ICGtesting.com
Printed in the USA
LVOW132140301012

305173LV00006B/48/P